Run Boy Run.

Roger Kendall

Chapter One. Easy Money.

'Oy you! Yes you, come here,' said the policeman walking over. A big man with a belt load of equipment. The boys stopped, surprised. They didn't dare move. Both had been lost in thought, Abdullah thinking about school and Ollie haunted by the image of his sister's frightened face.

He had visited her that morning and she had barely opened the door. The memory of her black eye, grazed cheek and the dirty marks of dried tears had stayed with him all day. Neither of them had noticed the fluttering police tape across the pavement.

'You with the frizzy hair empty your pockets, and the bag,' demanded the officer, 'and you too,' indicating Ollie.

Abdullah was clearly of African origin, and big for fourteen, but people found Ollie more difficult to label. Although his father was of mixed descent, Ollie took after his Anglo-Saxon Mother. Black wavy hair and white skin made him appear very English. His sister however was honey coloured and beautiful or she was when her boyfriend wasn't hitting her.

'Why, we haven't done anything?' exclaimed Ollie.

'Just effin do it.'

'What about some good manners?'

'Shut up,' whispered Abdullah to Ollie. 'It doesn't matter.'

'Just empty your pockets or you're in for it.'

'Going to Taser me, rather than say please? Or beat me with your stick,' said Ollie.

The policeman lunged but Ollie was good at running. It was that sort of neighbourhood. He slipped under the tape and ran up to a plain clothes policeman who was standing dejectedly by the blood stains.

'Hey, you can't go in there,' shouted the constable as he and a female officer moved quickly after Ollie.

'Excuse me but are you in charge?' said Ollie.

'At the moment but that tape means "keep out;" this is a crime scene,' said the detective.

'Sorry but your subordinate has been very rude and offensive; racially offensive.'

'My subordinate, you say,' he said, a slight smile hovering over his lips. 'We have to carry out searches you know. This is the fourth stabbing this week.'

'I know but that doesn't stop you being good mannered.'

'You'll still have to turn out your pockets.'

'I would be happy to if you ask properly. A please doesn't cost much does it? That's one of the problems here, offensive policemen.'

'Hey Roberts, this young man wants you to ask nicely.' The constable said nothing, just scowled.

'Would you please go behind the tape and please empty your pockets as my officer has requested,' said the detective.

Ollie went, put his bag down and fished out all the debris from his pockets which included a small penknife. The detective, who had followed him over, opened the knife, looked at Ollie, closed it and put it down on the growing pile.

'What's your name?'

'Ollie Lansbury.'

'And the bag, open it,' said the constable. Ollie, whose nerve was beginning to weaken, still managed to ignore the request. 'Please,' added the constable after some moments.

When the search was complete the constable went back to his post. As the boys walked away, the detective called Ollie back.

'I suppose you don't know anything about these stabbings or the way the gangs work or where the drugs come from?'

'No nothing.'

'Well, here's a card. If you hear anything ring me on that number, and if you can't get through, ring the general info line. This has to be stopped.' Ollie stared at the card.

'I wouldn't want this.'

'No, of course. Just put the numbers in your phone.'

Still Ollie hesitated. 'Put them down under my first name or DS or some other code.' With Ollie holding the card the detective went back to taking notes. The card felt like it would burn Ollie's fingers; could he just drop it in the gutter? Eventually after looking around, he slipped it into his pocket.

'Cor I'm still shaking,' said Ollie when he caught up with Abdullah around the next side street, a line of decent mews houses overshadowed by the blocks of council flats beyond. The 70's concrete eyesores stood like threatening monsters. Two older teenagers leaned against a wall watching them. It was a place to escape from.

Ollie had always wanted to find a better place, to be different, to speak better, not to be sucked into the sordid problems of the neighbourhood. He had reasoned that if he did well at school a good job might follow, but his greatest hope had been his sister. Everyone he knew fancied her and liked her. He had presumed she would find an educated boyfriend working in some prosperous company which he might later join but instead she was shacked up with some vicious thug. Somehow, he had to help her get away, but it is difficult when you are only fourteen.

'They were shaking too,' said Abdullah, interrupting Ollie's thoughts.

'Oh yeah.'

'They were, the copper was shaking with rage and the woman officer with suppressed laughter,' said Abdullah with a laugh.

'They shouldn't have been so rude.'

'What did he want you for?'

'Nothing.'

'I bet! You could get away with anything. They hardly searched your bag. If I'd had that knife, they'd have charged me. What did he say?'

'Wanted me to inform on the gangs.'

'Crazy, that's an invitation to a blade in the guts.'

'Yes,' he said looking at his trainers, 'but I don't know much anyway. Your brother's an addict, isn't he?'

'Yeah, tell me about it!' He used to do some running for the sellers, but they don't trust him now. He steals everything; drives my Mother mad. We can't keep anything safe in the house, TV, phones and he even stole an iron. How much do you get for an iron? Not enough for one spliff.'

'Why do people get involved with gangs and drugs?'

'Money, you can get £300 for going country.'

'£300! What do you have to do for that?' said Ollie a sudden idea giving hope.

'Pick up a package and take a train to some little town where you hand it over. My brother said it was easy. Trouble was it was too easy for him to skim some off. That's why they broke his fingers.'

'Ouch.'

'Danny has done it a couple of times.'

'Danny! He doesn't even look thirteen. He must look odd catching long distant trains.'

'No, cos he would do it at going home time, wearing school uniform. No one's going to check school-boys like us.'

'They just did, remember, but did he really receive £300?'

'Yup, though he didn't get paid immediate like. Had to do a second one but that was only Kingston,' said Abdullah, as they stopped outside the last of the Victorian semis where Ollie lived in an upstairs flat with his Mum.

'How would you find out who needs a runner?' said Ollie

'Don't be stupid. You are the one who was always going to get away. Always wanted to be posh, be different.'

'Yeah, but I need cash. Sasha's in trouble. Just one run would do it. I saw her this morning and her face looked like she'd done ten rounds with Mike Tyson.'

'I wouldn't risk it. Do your homework instead. Then you can help me do mine in tomorrow's break. See you,' said Abdullah as he strode off.

The following day, Ollie sought out Danny, a skinny boy who was only at school half the time. It was one of his school days and he appeared willing to talk.

'Yeh well, I sometimes do a country run,' he said.

'And you get £300?

'Mostly.'

'How did you find out about it?'

'Dunno really. My Mum's a heavy user. When there isn't any cash to pay for her poison, they get me to do a run,' said Danny.

'I need some money urgently; do you have a contact?'

'You sure you want to mix with them? You're the swot who doesn't know what happens on the street. Drugs are bad news unless you're the supplier.'

'I need some cash.'

'Ok, I'll ring someone. Give me your number. They'll ring you, cos that's the way it's done.'

In the mass afternoon-exodus Ollie, searched the crowded pavements. He had to avoid Abdullah for his worries were bad enough without censure from him. His own fears and conscience weighed heavily as he walked alone, even as others in school uniform pushed past. Passing the occasional groups of corner-hovering youths was worse. He was going to become one of them, compete, do a run for them, join their dangerous world. Just one run he told himself. It was a relief to reach the old green door of the flat and turn the key. Finally, home.

'Mum,' he said in startled surprise.

'You know Wednesdays are my new half day.'

'Sorry, just forgot.'

'You never told me how Sasha was when you took her, her coat? What she sees in that boy I don't know but as long as she's happy I suppose it's alright,' For one second Ollie wanted to confide in his mother but how could he tell her? Describe Sasha's battered face? He would have to be careful about what he said. Somehow if his sister's plight became known it would only make things worse.'

'I suppose you don't have any money I could borrow?' he said.

'No dear,' she laughed. If you look on the sideboard you will see a pile of unpaid bills. Never ahead, always behind, that's us. What do you want it for?'

'Nothing much.'

'You know you can tell me. I'm proud of how you're doing at school and Abdullah's a sensible friend. I know it's been hard since your father left but we are just managing.'

Nothing happened that night but at nine the following evening Ollie's very basic phone rang. The screen display read "caller unknown." Hesitatingly he answered it.

'You the white boy wanting to earn some readies?' said a West Indian voice with an East London twang.

'Err yes, please.'

'Four o'clock Waterloo tomorrow, back end of the taxi rank, bit of an underpass. Be in yer school uniform and 'ave a bag ready. Train to Guildford. They'll ring instructions on the way. Got it?

'I think so,' said Ollie suddenly acutely aware of what he was doing. A cold shiver ran through him. He expected the message to be repeated or his uncertainty questioned but there was just a click. He'd done it now. What would they do if he didn't turn up? But he needed the money; with his own cash savings he would have nearly £350, enough for Sasha to fly out to Spain and have a fresh start. She had a close friend working there so ought to be safe.

Leaving school after the afternoon break felt very strange. He glanced around the empty entrance; it had never seemed so large, the pavements so empty. He found the opposite on the underground where he imagined every eye was on him, all adults squashed together, he the only child, the only one in school uniform. Looking at the floor seemed safer but whenever he let his eyes look up, they met others, eyes full of questions before he looked away.

In the bustling echo of Waterloo, he felt alone, even as the crowds pushed past. At first, he was at the wrong entrance but then he found the taxi rank and the underpass. It was empty. He stood unsure. A businessman strode past and then three chattering nurses as he went to lean against the wall. A black teenager walked quickly through, flicked his finger at Ollie's bag and before it was hardly open, thrust a well filled paper bag in. Drugs! Feverishly Ollie glanced around. Someone must have seen; somehow it must have been spotted.

He joined a line in front of one of the ticket machines. Guildford. Where was that? As he clicked his way through the many instructions, he felt those behind him becoming impatient.

Finally, on the train, which was crowded, with people already standing, he needed to ease his wobbly legs. He pushed past. So many people, many in their twenties, most smartly dressed.

One man with white open shirt yet beautifully cut suit, brief case between his feet blocked the passage. He was leaning back nonchalantly on his arm, talking noisily to a shapely woman, also in a suit but with short skirt and high stilettos. An older businessman leant against the other side with an open newspaper. Ollie hesitated.

Finally, he muttered, 'Excuse me,' before brushing past the paper. He kept on walking, one carriage after another and then he saw a seat. A large woman had commandeered the aisle seat and had claimed the window seat with her coat and bag.

'Please,' said Ollie indicating the seat. Her only reply was a stony stare. 'Please.' The train jerked.

'Oh alright, - kids,' she muttered and pushing the bag under her seat, draped the coat over her ample lap, making the step through even more difficult but Ollie continued to hover until she shuffled her legs around so he could squeeze through. With his bag on his lap and her abundant flesh and coat overflowing onto him he began to feel hot and uneasy. He stared out of the window in embarrassment. The train was already stopping as it did again and again. How had he caught the slow train? His mobile rang, faces turned and stared. Deep within the seat confines it was ringing. Desperately he tried to reach it but by the time he had untangled it from his pocket, it had stopped.

He sat holding it waiting, and then its tone sounded loud and clear down the carriage.

'You on the train?'

'Yes but -'

'Back end of station, not the front, past shops, barbers, student walk to university, through old car park behind houses, at woods by uni. entrance. Got it?'

'Yeah, but it's a slow train.' The phone clicked dead.

Partly relieved he went through the instructions in his head. The train was slowing again, past a big house between mature trees, with new looking red brick walls broken up by cast stone window surrounds and fancy brickwork below the eaves. It was like some rich man's ancient house in Chelsea, yet it had garden all around it and it was new. A man on a sit-on mower was cutting the lawn and for a moment the sweet smell of cut grass floated through the doors as passengers disembarked. He saw there were another two houses but not quite the same, as if buyers expected individuality for their millions. As the train moved off, he saw more large houses, each in their own ample plot. And then the train was travelling past green fields, a cluster of smaller properties, barns, little areas of woodland, single oaks standing tall amidst the pastures, and horses.

How could you have enough money to live here and pay the fare to London every day? Was it boring, away from the city or was a walk in the fresh air enough? Did the very openness feel a threat or was it good not to be hemmed in by concrete?

The stations continued and finally Guildford. He jumped up and slowly the woman rose and gathered her coat.

'Excuse me,' he said, 'need to get off at Guildford.'

'Patience, it's London Road,' she said as he squeezed past.

'What do you mean? They said it was Guildford.'

'Yes, but not the main station. Don't you know where you're going?'

'Of course,' he mumbled, but he went and sat in an empty seat further back. The train started again and rumbled on to the main station. Stepping on to the platform he looked around but couldn't see the different entrances. Most travellers were in a rush but spotting someone standing waiting, he asked, and was directed across the bridge.

Coming out on to the pavement he stopped, and the flow of commuters around him threatened to knock him over. Putting the bag strap across his chest he looked around. Which way? No shops to the left, ah, a barber's, tucked in with other shops to the right. Three attractive girls walking together: students! He started off again, but the shops petered out. He looked down-side roads but there was no car park and then a small sign. More pretty girls and young Chinese men all looking fresh and affluent.

Following the sign, he came to a large scruffy car park with an old bus at one end. One side was the railway, the other a high wall but in the distance was a clump of trees, hardly a wood. His steps accelerated; at last he could be free of the package with all criminal evidence gone.

The sound of the motor bike didn't enter his consciousness until just before the tremendous jerk as the pillion rider grabbed his bag. Ollie flew into the pillion rider, who nearly fell off the bike as they thudded together. Putting his hands out as he fell, Ollie managed to avoid the spokes of the bike as it did a spurt of acceleration, but even as the bag was being pulled over his head he hung on.

He was on hands and knees when his assailant slid off the back of the bike and kneed him in the face, jerking at the bag again as he did so. Then, yanking a handful of Ollie's jacket, he flung him on to his back. Ollie rolled, expecting a further kicking when his hold on the bag's strap finally broke and the pillion rider ran the few paces to the bike, and jumped on to it as it accelerated away in a shower of gravel.

Ollie lay there gasping for breath as a feeling of dread surged over him. He delayed opening his eyes but when he heard voices, he looked up to see a Chinese girl staring down at him.

'You Ok?' she said. A second girl was gazing at her phone. 'My friend ring police.'

'No,' he said jumping to his feet but stumbling with pain, 'no don't ring them, I'm alright, please don't.'

'But we saw it. Why not?'

'I dunno but don't,' he said limping away as quickly as he could. When he reached the road. he had to stop and lean against a fence. Gasping for each painful breath he stared about him, the white fear of what his suppliers would do etched on his face. Overcoming indecision, he hobbled back to the station.

When he finally caught a train, he collapsed into one of the many empty seats and waited for the call. It came.

'I've been robbed,' he said, trying to get it in first.

A string of obscenities and then, 'you owe us two grand. You'd better have it by the end of the week, or you're barbecued.'

'Someone must have known. They were waiting for me.'

'Oh yeah, you lost it. Your stupid fault.'

'I never told anyone.'

'Must've. Two grand, get it.'

He leaned back in the seat and tried to stop the tears that were welling up within him. Stupid, why had he been so stupid? He should have been looking out for trouble. Everything was ruined, what could he do? They knew he had no money. What was he supposed to do, steal it, and from where? He wiped his eyes and realised the graze on his hand was bleeding. Using a little tissue, he tried to clean his face and then his hand, but the tissues crumbled into red and white confetti. A woman further up the carriage was watching him with a matronly expression of concern. Somehow sympathy was the last thing he wanted. Giving an involuntary sob he turned and stared out of the window. A station flashed by.

A fast train! He didn't need to go all the way to Waterloo, did he? Where could he join the local train? But the map tucked in his bag had gone. School library book, calculator, pens and exercise books all gone! Finished work all lost; what was he to do?

Chapter two. Debt.

The following day was Saturday and although he had homework, he found it difficult to concentrate and even after a call to Abdullah he didn't have adequate information to complete much. The breadknife, their only large blade, gave little comfort, even as he carried it from room to room, checking the door every time he passed. The evening before, by a quick rush to the bathroom and a careful turning of his face, he had managed to avoid his injuries being seen by his mother. She left for work early on Saturday and later by staying in his room Ollie's facial grazing remained unnoticed.

On Sunday he was determined to stay in and quickly took a late breakfast back to his room.

'Forgot to buy enough milk. Pop down to the shop and get four pints can you, Ollie?' said his Mum through the door.

'I've homework to finish.'

'Only take you ten minutes,'

'But -.'

'No buts, come on,' she said giving his door a knock and entering, purse in hand. 'What an earth has happened to your face, and the bread knife, what's that doing here?'

He stared up at his mother. 'I fell over, it's nothing.'

'Let me look,' she said, but he turned his head away.

'And your hand? What have you put on it?'

'Don't fuss, I'm alright and I put Dettol on it.'

'Is that's why you are hiding in here?'

'It's my room.'

'It doesn't stop you going to the shops, - or does it? What's going on?'

'Nothing!'

'Then you can go, can't you?'

'Yeah alright.' He said glancing at his watch. Perhaps ten o'clock Sunday morning wasn't the time for gang members to be around. 'Shut the door then.'

He was careful to make sure his trainers were tight and that the knife up his sleeve wouldn't prevent him running fast. At the outside door he stared down the street and hesitated before stepping on to the pavement and in an anxious, head turning looking everyway walk, hurried to the Tesco local. The streets felt threatening in their quietness, but he saw no one who looked a danger, until he reached the shop. A tall youth of Pakistani origin was inspecting the snacks. Ollie backed away, his eyes never leaving the youth's face. Reaching the milk, he grabbed a container and quickly operated a self-service checkout before hurrying away. As he neared his home he broke into an involuntary run. Panting he slammed into the door and then couldn't get his key out.

The door opened. 'What's the noise Ollie? And we never have full fat milk.'

'Oh sorry, I didn't look.'

'Are you being bullied? Bullying is a serious matter, and your school has some sort of system doesn't it? Come on, you can tell me.'

'Look, it's nothing I can't sort out,' he lied, pushing past. For the rest of the day, he stayed in his room except for mealtimes where he tried to read in the sullen silence and avoid his mother's occasional probing question.

On Monday he was slow to rise.

'I don't feel well,' he said entering the kitchen and slumping on a stall. Disturbed sleep and nightmares had left him tired and wan, so he hoped he actually looked ill.

'I'll walk you to school then, to make sure you are Ok,' said his mother.

'You what, you can't do that.'

'If you are being picked on, they'll have to pick on me too.'

'You'd make me a laughingstock.'

'So, better than being beaten up. You could always tell me about it instead.'

'Alright,' he said snatching up whatever books and kit he still had and sweeping it into an old sports bag.

'Where's your normal bag?' she said, 'and what about your breakfast?'

'I lost it,' he said slamming the door.

Out on the pavement he hurried, constantly turning his head, his anger overcoming his fear for the moment. Reaching the school his fear returned and continued throughout the day, but nothing happened. As the end of the afternoon approached, his lack of weapon worried him. No shop was going to sell him a knife and the nearest DIY shop where he might buy a screwdriver was miles away. Then he saw that a maintenance man was at work, rehanging a door, a toolbox beside him. As he walked past Ollie kicked a mallet sliding it along the floor. Picking it up he went to put it back in the box. The man turned away as Ollie clattered it back in, but he palmed a medium screwdriver in exchange. With short, guilt-strained breaths he hurried away.

Finally, after running home, he sat exhausted on his bed turning the screwdriver in his hand and wandering what was happening to him. He'd never pinched sweets at the local shops like some of his friends but now he had robbed someone of the tools of his trade. He tried to justify his need. No doubt they could afford it and he had no choice; he had to be armed. It was a useful size, small enough to hide but big enough to frighten an attacker. Tomorrow he would sharpen the end on a concrete kerb.

The following day, no one followed or threatened him, but the endless fear wore him down and his schoolwork suffered. In the evening as he tried to concentrate the phone rang. He answered automatically.

'Where's the cash? Tomorrow you start paying. You screw up this time and you're history. Same place but later at 5pm, train to Hastings. Got it?'

'But the fare -,' the phone clicked dead. The call he had feared strangely brought relief. However long it took, they would let him pay it off. He went to the little drawer that held his savings and a post office book. He counted the cash £26.52. Probably enough for this trip but only just. The savings account held £45 but he wasn't sure how he could get it out?

Crossing the concourse at Waterloo his nerves returned as two police officers stood observing the mass of flowing commuters. A man in plain clothes joined them. Ollie saw that it was the detective who had been at the murder scene. Who were they looking for and would the detective recognise him? If he were stopped would the screwdriver be thought of as a weapon? Perhaps it was better that he hadn't had time to sharpen it. He continued to head down to cross the vast space as boldly as he could, but most people were going the other way. Two businessmen in animated conversation walked straight at him. Looking up, he just dodged them, but he brushed against one of them who snarled his displeasure.

'Look where you are going boy!'

Ollie saw the detective was looking at him. The man nodded and smiled but there was also an observant curiosity in his look. Ollie kept walking, his knees like jelly. When he reached the underpass, he slumped against the wall breathing heavily, reeking of his own sweat. He couldn't go back through the station. Perhaps the run might be called off and he could ditch the screwdriver, but his hopes faded as an Asian boy as young as himself but with a cocky "who cares" swagger was approaching him. He handed him a rolled supermarket bag.

'Cops about,' he said as he sauntered off. Ollie shoved it into his bag with trembling fingers aware of the constant flow of commuters all of whom must have seen the exchange.

'Stupid,' he muttered to himself. He hardly had the energy to move but he knew he had to. Walking back round the outer edge of the concourse he looked for the police but couldn't see them.

He reached the stairs to a first-floor café. By going up the stairs he could have a full view of the station. In the hubbub of the self-service Pret-a-Manger, his thumping heartbeat began to slow. Unnoticed he could watch. The police were still there but on the other side of the W.H. Smith's outlet. Somehow, he had to avoid them, yet read the train times on the great electronic board and buy a ticket. It felt impossible and he continued to stand rigid, frozen in indecision.

Suddenly the lounging police came alive as a young man walked through the barriers. Shocked, the man stood uncertain as they closed around him. He walked off with them but as there had been no scuffle, the arrest went unnoticed by most travellers. Ollie gulped. At least he could now leave but the way that the police had been waiting for their man was a reminder of the risks he took. Glancing at his watch he realised he was going to be late. Quickly he ran down the stairs and joined those staring at the board, but Hastings wasn't on it.

'Excuse me,' he said to a uniformed railway man walking through. 'How do I get to Hastings?'

'Not sure but you need to get to Charing Cross first.'

After 45 minutes of anxious research, ticket selection, running up escalators and squeezing into tube trains he caught a Hastings train. It was crowded but he found an out of the way corner to lean against. He breathed out with relief. His phone rang.

'You on the train?' demanded the voice.

'Only just.'

'Ten Cornwallis Drive; basement flat. Give it to Jo, no one else. Got it?'

'Yes, 10 Cornwallis Drive, Jo.' The phone clicked.

After the train had stopped at a second station, he was able to find a seat. His phone rang again. Looking down he saw it was his mother's number. He'd started his travels later, so it was already 6pm. He let it ring. What could he say? He could tell her he was at

Abdullah's, but he was fed up with lying and she could easily check.

When it rang a second time, he was ready.

'Hi Mum, sorry I forgot. I'm helping out my friend Danny so won't be back till about 9pm.'

'What about your tea then?'

'Can I have it when I'm back?'

'Of course, I'll plate it up and you can microwave it. Who's Danny, and what are you doing exactly?' For a moment he couldn't hear her as there was the air horn blast of a passing train.

'What was that noise?'

'Just the TV, but I must go,' he said ending the call. He sat, despondently looking out at the countryside. Why must his mother ask so many questions? He tried to cool the anger which boiled within him. He knew he shouldn't blame her. It was his sister's fault for getting in with such a brute, or his father's fault for leaving them, but mainly his own, his stupidity that the stuff had been stolen. Why hadn't he been more alert? This time he would be ready. He felt the smooth handle of the screwdriver, the steel blade cold against his leg, yet if he stabbed someone, the whole situation could become even worse. The countryside looked just as attractive, but it was an alien world. A place he would never get to know. His dreams of good grades, followed by a well-paid job, were going down the drain. The journey seemed to go on for ever.

The train finally rolled into the station and with no map he had to ask passers-by outside. A matronly woman pointed out the direction. He surveyed every corner, and turned to watch every moving vehicle, his ears and eyes alert to everything out of the ordinary as he walked the short distance to the address. It was in a line of town houses most of which were in reasonable condition although the basement flat of number ten, had dead plants and two rusting car wheels amongst other detritus around the steps down into it.

He knocked. A middle-aged white man half opened the door and peered round, unshaven, a roll up dangling from his lips. 'Yeah wod-do-you want?'

'You Jo?'

'Could be. You got something for me or you buying?'

'Are you Jo?'

'Yeah. Better hand it over.'

With a last look round, Ollie eased out the parcel in its rolled-up supermarket bag and gave it to the man. He went to close the door, but Ollie just stood there.

'What you waiting for? A receipt? Hoppit.' The door slammed.

Emerging onto the pavement Ollie hurried back to the station. There was a long wait for the next train. In the warm waiting room, he stared at the rows of iced buns. He licked his dry lips. His hand went to his pocket, but the coins felt too few and vital to waste. Back on the cold platform the hunger gnawed at his empty stomach and the unfairness ground around his mind.

His mother was busy watching TV when he returned so he was able to deflect her questions easily. Tired he fell asleep much quicker than expected but woke at 4am. with the situation running a circle of worry in his brain. His mind was still numb when he sat down by Abdullah in class.

'Have you done the math's homework yet?' asked Abdullah.

'Eh no.'

'It's got to be in by Thursday.'

'Some chance.'

'But I thought you would be able to understand it. You normally do it before anyone else.'

'Yeah, well, bit behind now. I'll look later,' he said. Perhaps by then the brain deadening tiredness would have worn off, he thought. And after tea that evening it had. He forgot his problems as he wrestled with the difficult maths but then his phone rang.

'Where's the money?' demanded the voice. With a glance at his mother, Ollie hurried to his bedroom as the caller continued to give instructions.

'What did you say?'

'I need the rest of the money.'

'But I went to Hastings.'

'Yeah that just covers the interest. Birmingham tomorrow, pick up 47 South Street, near yer school.'

'But I've no money for the fare.'

'Your problem.'

'It's yours if I get stopped because I've no ticket.'

'Look you little doad. You get your own travel cash.'

'But I can't.'

'Alright, you touch the main packet and you're toast but there'll be an extra bung in an envelope, gives you fifty quid if you sell right.'

'But I can't -.'

'You're in the business now. Keep the punters happy. Just weed, plenty of kids in your school like a bit.'

'But -.' The phone clicked.

He stared down at the screen, running his fingers over the buttons. How could he sell marijuana to his friends?

South Street was a small group of council houses, overshadowed by later high-rise flats. Forgotten and forlorn, broken toys and the remains of bathroom fittings long since replaced, littered the small front gardens. Number 47 was the second house on the street, the previous numbers having been demolished to make way for the flats. Ollie hesitated at the broken gate. He gulped but finally walked over the carpet of cigarette ends to the door. The bell push was missing from its surround and there was no knocker, but the door swung open. A tall black youth put his head round the door, glanced up the road and jerked his finger for Ollie to enter. Stepping around a broken vacuum, Ollie saw an elderly, obese woman watching him from a modern armchair.

'Come here boy,' she said, hooking her nicotine stained finger at him. 'Closer. You owe me, yet spect me to pay your ticket. You mess with us and you're history.'

He heard a movement behind him but before Ollie could turn, an arm was round his neck and the youth's other hand was attempting to twist Ollie's right arm around. Much as he resisted, the older lad was much stronger and bore Ollie downwards and the twisted arm hurt. His head was suddenly released, and he was propelled across the floor, sliding to the foot of the armchair. A hand grabbed his hair, jerking his head up. The woman leaned down her face close to his.

'Got it?'

'Yes,' he managed.

'Watch you do. There's some weed in the bag. Plenty of cash at a two quid a go. They'll ring, Birmingham New Street.'

Ollie looked around.

'It ain't kept here,' she said and started texting on her phone. Ollie just stood there easing his stiff neck around. The black youth said nothing but stared coldly at Ollie. The front door opened, and a black man entered, his crinkly hair grey at the edges. He glanced at the woman and when she nodded, passed Ollie a large McDonald's bag.

'You want me to go tonight?'

'Yeah, course' said the new arrival, grabbing a handful of Ollie's sweatshirt and propelling him towards the door. 'Straight there.' Ollie stumbled to the door but steadied himself and leaned against the frame. He wanted to be sick. 'What you waiting for?'

'I- I've no cash for the fare,' he finally said.

'He's got some weed to sell,' said the woman.

'What nothing?' said the older man.

'No, nothing.'

'Give him some dough, you stupid cow,' said the man and then pulled out a thick wad of notes and peeled off two twenty-pound notes. 'Use the dope for the next one, now get going.'

As he neared the station, he passed a group of mainly black teenagers who stared at him. The big take-away packet was too large for his shoulder bag and was threatening to pop out. His hand closed on the screwdriver. Was he in a different patch? He knew he shouldn't stare back at them, but he couldn't help it. He quickened his pace. One of them laughed. Another one jumped towards Ollie and they all laughed as he broke into a run.

In the station he stared at the maps, so jittery the diagrams were just a blur. Eventually he joined a queue in front of a cashier's window. Taking deep breaths, he tried to calm himself. 'I need to get to Birmingham, please. A ticket to whatever station I need,' he said when his turn came.

On the underground he managed to get a seat and sat numb, despondently hunched, not noticing the mass of travellers who flowed in and out as the train stopped and started its way across London. At Euston he should have been pleased to have quickly caught a fast train, but he remained stunned, staring at the grey seatback in front. As people walked past his aisle seat, he neither saw them nor took any interest in them.

His phone rang. Answering it automatically, he waited for the crude, minimal instructions.

'Easy one kid,' said the voice. Costa in the station, little side entrance. Meet there. Wait for your contact. Got it?' the same voice but not of anyone he had met at the house.

'Ok,' said Ollie. As the call ended, he saw that a woman dressed as a nun was looking at him. A second nun was sitting beside her; real nuns. He had seen pictures of nuns but never seen one live. A different era; what were their lives like? Did any of them feel trapped too? Or did they feel safe mostly away from the world.

It was a long journey but at least he was safe on the train. His interest in the city and then the countryside began to return as he watched it flash past. He tried to forget his violent masters and what he owed them. This time he had already made his excuses to his mother and had even persuaded her to make him sandwiches. Glancing around to make sure no one was watching; he took out the take-away bag and looked in. At the top was a bulky, plastic bag full of plant material and at the bottom a second, compactly filled bag. He took out some homework but every time he tried to concentrate, he saw the woman's face as she twisted his hair and gave him his orders in a shower of spittle.

He stood and went to the toilet compartment where he splashed his face and vigorously rubbed his hands in an attempt to feel clean again. It wasn't enough to allow him to focus on his homework, but he managed to eat his sandwich without noticing what he was eating.

At Birmingham's station when going from smart shop to shop he couldn't help but look up and marvel at the modern building. Somehow it made him feel better. When he found the coffee shop, he squatted down in a corner outside to wait. The minutes ticked by and nobody came. He stretched, wandered over to Smiths which was next door and stood reading the headlines until he noticed the cashier staring at him. Returning to Costa he paced up and down, glancing at his watch, constantly looking out for likely contacts. A blonde youth approached, glancing around. He flicked his head to remove a hank of hair that half covered his eyes. The dark circles below and grazed cheek of someone living badly. He flicked his fringe again, all part of constant jittery movements.

'You from London?' Ollie nodded. The youth reached out, took the MacDonald's bag and hurried away.

Ollie felt relieved, until he remembered, he still had enough weed to get him put away in a young offender's centre. It was the early hours of the morning before his feet echoed hurriedly down the dark streets to his home.

The following evening, he heard his phone ring, but it was in his bedroom, so by the time he reached it, it had stopped. He was relieved that he had missed their call and when it rang again the following night, he let it ring. He was still too tired to even consider a run and the drugs remained unsold, hidden at home. He told himself he didn't care anymore but later he began to fear what he had done. If he had been able, he would have rung them back. The dread began to grow.

Three days later, returning from school he stopped at the outer doorway to the flats and turned to wave goodbye to Abdullah. A youth stepped up from the basement steps beside him. He was over six-foot-tall, yet his brown skin was smooth as a baby, with only the slightest fuzz decorating his top lip.

'Maggie wants to see you.'

'I've too much homework. I'll see her next week,' said Ollie guessing that she was the woman at number 47.

The scuff of a step behind him and then a whack in the back, where someone shoved him hard. Stumbling across the paving he turned. There were two other black youths behind him.

'Huh, Maggie doesn't wait for little idiots like you. Move,' said the one in front of the door, giving Ollie a push on his shoulder. They closed round him. A swish sound as a piece of concrete narrowly missed them to thud against the door. Abdullah was already easing another piece of mortar out of a neighbour's crumbling brick wall, even as he looked poised to run. They all ducked as the second piece whizzed past and ricocheted off the house.

'Get him,' shouted the tall lad, just before Ollie hit him hard in the stomach. He doubled up gasping for air. Ollie shouldered his way past. His key was in the door and half turned when the lad grabbed his collar with one hand and punched the side of his head with the other. The door opened and they thudded onto the mat to the sound of the others running down the street. Ollie tried to drag himself to the stairs, praying someone would hear the disturbance but there were only six flats apart from the basement and nobody came. The door slammed behind them. Ollie was hit again but even as the lad hung on to him, he dragged him to the stairs.

Suddenly Ollie was released but, before he could get up, a large boot kicked his thigh. Turning over, he was ready to spring up or catch a flying foot but the big lad, just stood towering over him. He glanced at the nearest flat doors.

'Next time I'll have a knife,' he hissed.

'I haven't sold the weed yet. I promise to do another run when I have. Tell her that.'

'Nobody tells her. You either come or you're dead.'

'Alright but first I must put my bag inside.'

'You think I'm stupid?'

'No, I promise. I don't want you coming back, do I?' said Ollie, bumping his bottom up the first steps and then standing.

They glared at each other. One of the others was banging on the outside door which had slammed shut. Turning Ollie ran up the stairs and tossed his bag into his home. He stood and looked down the stairs, his face pinched and white, frozen in indecision. The flat had never felt so welcoming, the temptation to run inside and slam the door, shutting out the danger of even more pain was too much, but he knew it was his last chance. If he didn't go with them, they might even kill him.

'Just a moment,' Ollie shouted running into his bedroom but deliberately leaving the flat door open. He knew, once it was closed, he would be too frightened to open it again. Finding the screwdriver, he slipped it into his pocket and taking a deep breath, limped slowly down the stairs. His head hurt but his assailant, who was now standing holding the main door open, had been hurt too.

'Keep your mates away.'

The other two were hovering outside but they made no attempt to attack Ollie.

'She'll eat you,' one of them said.

'Yeah, cut you up as rat bait.'

It was the faltering steps of the condemned going to the scaffold. By the time they had reached number 47, only the tall boy accompanied him who pushed past and rapped on the door with his knuckles. The door opened and Maggie was sitting there in the same chair as if she hadn't moved from the week before. Her minder was also the same, but Ollie side-stepped and made sure he could see both him and the lad who had brought him.

'I, I'm sorry I couldn't come.'

'You'll be a lot sorrier if you mess with me. You answer the phone when I ring,' she spat. 'What happened to the grass?'

'I haven't had time to sell it.'

'You what! I didn't give it to you to rot under your bed.'

'Sorry.'

'Where's your bag?' she said, looking at the lad who had brought him.

'At home.'

'Useless! Find him a bag,' she said gesturing to her minder who ran up the stairs to return with an old sports bag. She began texting but added 'Downs run, Brighton. You'll have to find the way.'

'What, now?'

'Yeah urgent.'

There was a tap on the door. The minder looked out the window and let the new arrival in, who went straight to Maggie and whispered in her ear. He looked like a young black boxer, slim hips and wide shoulders. Ollie bent his head and looked away. He didn't want to be recognised. This was Todd Osbourne, Sasha's boyfriend. Maggie was texting again. Even in the corner, rubbing his forehead in an effort to hide his face Ollie expected to be recognised but the hated boyfriend just looked through him as they all waited. The same older man arrived, handed a package to Ollie and then a smaller one to Todd and walked through to a back room without comment. Todd turned and left but hesitated at the door and gave a last glance at Ollie.

'I suppose you've got no money,' said Maggie fishing out two twenty-pound notes from where they were wedged between her hips and the arm of the chair.

Ollie was still repeating the address as he left the house, but Todd was waiting.

'You're Sasha's brother, aren't you?'

'Yeah so?'

'What you doing here then? Don't go flogging any stuff over other side of the A23 or you'll be in the Somali's patch and they don't take prisoners,' said Todd.

'Is that where you sell it?'

'None of your business. This is just a bit of stuff for some friends,' said Todd walking away.

Ollie exhaled. A trip to Brighton was annoying but at least he was unhurt, and he'd showed he wasn't a pushover, but he'd pushed his luck. He shuddered at what might have happened. His captor emerged from the house behind him.

'You'd better get going,' he said.

'Why aren't you doing it?'

'Less chance of you being stopped with your white skin. I'm like your local supplier.'

'Where does he fit in?' said Ollie pointing to where Todd was just driving his BMW off the pavement.

'You'll not last long if you stick your nose in.'

'I know him from somewhere else.'

'Aren't you lucky? If you wind Maggie up, you might see him one last time.'

Chapter three. The Boyfriend.

He caught the train without trouble and leaned back comfortably on one of the last free seats, pleased at the confident way he had bought the right ticket and found the train. The ticket machines were no longer the enemy trying to embarrass him in front of a line of commuters, and he had felt at ease being swept along with the office workers in their homeward rush. He idly flicked through a free newspaper that had been left on the seat but then he remembered the look Todd had given him.

Was he really some sort of hit man as well as a nightclub bouncer? He was certainly violent enough. How could he ever rescue Sasha from a man like that? If Todd came after him, he'd be mincemeat. Trying to push the fear out of his mind, he concentrated on the journey and where he had to go. He repeated the Brighton address and directions to himself. Sounded easy and then his glance fell on a news item in the paper. A drug gang had been convicted and its county line mules sent to prison for three and four years. A chill went through him and he found he was slipping down the seat in an unconscious attempt to become invisible. The length of sentences was terrifying. Was what he was doing really that serious?

The fug in his head from his fear of being caught only dissipated as he alighted at the busy station and in the effort to find the house. When he did, the door was partially open, so he stepped inside, nearly tripping over a pair of white legs in laddered fishnet stockings. The bleary-eyed woman on the floor, possibly once attractive but no more, stared up at him. A man came into the hall, saw Ollie and lurched towards him.

'You got the stuff?'

The dilated pupils and jittery stance didn't encourage conversation, so Ollie pushed passed. In any case he was supposed to ask for a woman. He looked in at the first doorway.

'Is Jenny here?' he enquired of the large room, once elegant with Edwardian coving and stripped wallpaper but the chandelier had been stolen, to be replaced by a single light bulb which dangled on a long flex. The dismal light threw shadows on the torn and faded walls as a woman and man rose from the floor. Others just stared up at Ollie or remained curled up in their dirty sleeping bags. A strong aroma of unwashed bodies, damp plaster and curry made his nostrils contract.

'I'm Jenny,' said the woman but her companions' sudden glance said otherwise.

'Where is she?'

'She'll come but you got to give us the stuff,' said the man half hidden under the dirty blanket around his shoulders. It was difficult to judge his age. He looked ancient but Ollie guessed he was probably only thirty. Another person rose, sliding up the wall for support. The boy should have felt threatened by the desperate adults waiting for their fix, but their hovering was more pathetic than dangerous.

'I'll wait,' said Ollie looking round for somewhere clean. Another man came in.

'You from London?' he said coming close as if to take the bag. Ollie moved quickly, brushing past. A grabbing hand reached for him but wasn't quick enough to catch the boy who weaved through them.

'I'll wait outside.'

He went and lent against a wall. The three-storey house from outside looked unkempt but otherwise normal, nothing to tell passers-by that it was full of addicts. He noticed a man was watching him from the other side of the street. A woman was walking briskly down the street towards him. She stopped and handed him a package and then stood in front of him as if to hide what he was doing. Something fluttered onto the pavement. A twenty-pound note; they were counting money! She turned and crossed the street.

'I'm Jenny, you delivering?' she said.

'Yes,' said Ollie, looking at the man, who nodded to him before turning and walking to a dark Mercedes. Ollie handed over the package and with a last glance at the house walked away.

When he could finally slump back into the seat cushions of the train he soon began to doze, to awake with a start. Images of a giant Todd had leaned over him, like some mighty genie, swinging his fists. In the dream which continued to whirl around in his head he had seen a screaming Sasha trying to intervene and being hit again and again in Ollie's place. He trembled. How had they ended up in such a mess? What chance was there that they could sort it? The confidence from a satisfactory delivery seeped away as his worries echoed the rumble of the train. Somehow, he had to think through what chances he had. But they all needed money.

His phone pinged, a text from Abdullah. He'd forgotten him.

'You Okay? Those yobs chased me for half a mile,' it said.

Rubbing his thigh, which still hurt, he texted back.

'Thanks for the bricks, glad you got away all right. All explained tomorrow. You saved my butt,' he texted.

At school the following day in the first break he sought out Danny, who he knew was still involved somehow with drugs, but he was busy talking to another lad and two girls. Ollie hovered nearby but Danny was too busy laughing with the others. Finally, they broke up and Danny walked over.

'You look tired mate. Told you not to mix with them, not good for your health.'

'How did you know?'

'I hear most stuff that goes on.'

'I need some cash. Do you know who might want to buy some of this,' said Ollie pulling a small plastic bag of cannabis out of his pocket.

'You're crazy man,' said Danny looking around nervously. 'You'll get kicked out if they catch you.'

'It's just the one lot I need to sell,' said Ollie his own eyes flicking around the busy playground.

'Yeah looks alright,' said Danny taking the bag and keeping it in the palm of his hand so it couldn't be seen, opened it and sniffed. 'Okay, bit dry, best place is down the park at lunchtime but watch your back. What happened to your delivery cash?'

'Got robbed, so I owe them.'

'Turned you over did they? Old trick that one; warned you.' A bell rang in the distance.

'You don't want to buy any?'

'Naw, plenty at home if I need some. Watch out down the park, it's really Somali territory' said Danny walking away.

Ollie was still standing there as others hurried to their classes.

'Hey,' said Abdullah approaching him. 'You glued to the playground? Old Pecker will get humpty if you're late. You don't look too beaten up?' Ollie just shrugged and followed him.

'Yeah thanks to you. What are you doing after school? I might need a bit of help?'

'As long as it's not taking on that lot. What's got you into mixing with guys like that?'

'It's a long story,' said Ollie but by then they were walking down the corridor with everyone else. 'Tell you tonight; meet at the park, five o'clock.'

The park on a noisy road junction wasn't much more than a toddler's fenced off playground, a small area of tarmac around a single basketball stand and a couple of park seats in front of a group of trees. The shrubbery around the trees had long been trampled back to bare earth. Ollie was sitting on one of the swings watching a crowd of youths around the park seats. The swing was rather tight. The movement of a high sided truck on the road caused the take-away bags to flutter at his feet.

He counted three girls and seven lads. Most were from year ten or eleven. They were just chatting, except one boy who was practicing vaulting over a seat as if it was a future Olympic sport. Another lad lit a cigarette and passed it to one of the girls. Her honey-coloured skin reminded him of Sasha. She took a puff and passed it on. Someone else put his hand out and it was passed to him. Further cigarettes were being lit. As far as Ollie could see they were normal tobacco. He checked his phone. No reply from Abdullah and then as he started to text him, he entered the playground.

'Hi,' he said squeezing into the other swing. 'So, what have you got yourself into?'

Ollie briefly told him the story of his first run and robbery. 'I think now, it was the pushers who set me up, robbing me of their own stuff so they wouldn't have to pay me. That's what Danny's suggested. They are sending me all over the place. That's the gang that grabbed me outside our flat.'

'What are you going to do?'

'What can I do? I was so scared yesterday that they were really going to cripple me. I'm trapped. I just have to go on.'

'You'll get caught by the old bill if they don't kill you. Don't involve me, just get out. Next time I might not be able to run fast enough. They're all bigger than us.'

'I just need you to watch my back, be a minder, I have to sell some cannabis. I just you need you -.'

'You're selling the stuff?'

'Yeah, just a one off, I hope. Please, just be a lookout. Shout if you see police or other nasties.'

'What here, now?' said Abdullah looking round.

'Need to try. I think the drug can go off. Has a sort of sell-by date.'

'You up to your eyes in this and you don't know the first thing about the business, do you?'

'Not really,' Ollie sighed, 'Do you think that lot might want some?'

'Could do. You see the one sitting on the bench. What he's rolling aint no tobacco.'

Ollie breathed out and stood. Still, he hesitated.

'I'll go and stand at the corner,' said Abdullah pointing to the junction between two roads. 'It's close enough that you'll hear me, but I can leg it if I have too.'

'That's not exactly a backup but alright,' said Ollie walking on. He supposed he couldn't blame Abdullah for not wanting to get too close. The group didn't appear to notice him even when he was standing right in front of them. Eventually one of the girls nodded.

'What ya staring at kid?' said the girl blowing smoke over him.

'Got some good gear. Wondered if you wanted to buy?'

'Oh yeah, been robbing the nursery, have you?'

'Naw, left over stuff; it's kosher. Want to try a bit?' said Ollie with a slight gulp as they had begun to gather around in a tight semicircle. Even the seat vaulter had stopped, sitting down on the top of the seatback, with his feet on the seat he leaned over the others.

'Kids like you should be home with your mummy,' said the same girl. She was darker than the rest, her hair with its extensions woven into cornrow plaits, complete with colourful cottons.

'Start young these days,' said a big white lad. 'So, what you got?' Ollie handed over a small bag of cannabis. The lad opened it and sniffed it. 'Free sample is it?'

'No, you pay for it, two quid a bag. It's good stuff.' The lad's eyebrows went up.

'Got much?'

'Enough.'

'Ok, I'll have a fiver's worth then.'

'Yes Okay,' said Ollie trying not to show his surprise but he did hold his hand out for the money before he found three bags in his over-stuffed pockets. 'Three for a fiver then.' He looked around at the others who just stared. 'Anybody else?'

'Yeah, alright I'll have three,' said another boy.

'Waste of money,' said the girl with the plaits. 'The boys from Balham will kill you if they see you dealing on their patch.'

'Leave him alone. He's only a kid,' said the honey-coloured girl.

'Lend me some money and I'll have some.' said another boy but nobody offered. A further boy rattled two pounds in his hand and took a bag. They went back to their conversations ignoring Ollie, but he was feeling pleased as he walked away. Nobody had attacked him, he had twelve pounds in his pocket and some of the cannabis had gone.

There was a shrill whistle. He looked up vaguely and then saw Abdullah was waving. About ten, mainly black youths, were walking down the road to the park. For a moment, Ollie thought 'more customers' but then he looked again; they were a swaggering, strutting group, spreading their bravado across the full width of the pavement. A mother and daughter stepped into the road out of their way. One lad was kicking a drinks can, another tossed a bottle into a nearby garden. Heads high, they were looking around as if daring combat. Turning, Ollie crossed the road. He knew he shouldn't run but he couldn't stop his legs. A fast walk became a run. Glancing back, he saw they weren't following but they were watching him. 'Stupid,' he muttered between his heavy breaths as he slowed to a walk.

It took him some time to circle round the side streets back to Abdullah who had texted to say he was at McDonalds. He found him sitting inside playing on his phone.

'Want a coke?' said Abdullah, lifting his own cup.

'Got to save my money.'

'Come on, didn't you sell any?'

'Yup, got rid of some of it,' said Ollie glancing around, remembering that his pockets still contained enough little packets to get him convicted as a pusher. The café was busy; a group of teenagers in a queue were pushing and shoving in a good-natured way. Several older student types were clicking their orders on the order pads. A couple of overall clad workmen were reading newspapers. He didn't think any of them would use cannabis. 'I wonder who that lot were?'

'Probably the Balham gang. You were on their patch. Did they notice you?'

'Might have done,' said Ollie, not wanting to admit it. He took a sip of Abdullah's coke. 'I've still got a lot to get rid of. Your brother Nadeem doesn't want any?'

'No, not now; Nadeem's a registered addict so he gets methadone at some clinic. He even had a job for a while but then he lost it again. Sort of in a spin-cycle. One day he's clean, next he's nicking stuff to pay for more dope. Weed was never his poison. What about Agers? His friends use the stuff.'

'You know where he lives?'

'Yeah,' said Abdullah taking a long swig. 'Finish it up.' Ollie drained the beaker and followed his friend outside. He caught up with him as he strode on. 'Need to get home soon but we'll find him first.'

The property at the end of the row of council houses had been extended and looked smarter than the rest. The original front garden had been recently surfaced with new pavers. The door opened to Abdullah's knock.

'You after Smithy?' said the big white teenager who opened the door. Only the shiny black hair revealed some previous family connection to the Indian continent. Heavy metal music thumped the air.

'No Agers, I suppose it's you we want. Ollie reckons you might need some decent weed,' said Abdullah, indicating Ollie over his shoulder.

'Yeah come in, everybody else is here,' said Agers leading them into a side room which once must have been a double garage but was now carpeted with bean bags and settees.

Ollie was surprised to see several of his classmates and a couple of lads he didn't know lounging on the sofas and floor. The aroma of cannabis and tobacco mingled with take away pizza. Several boxes lay on the floor each with an odd slice left. Tins of lager and coke were scattered about. His stomach reminded him he ought to be going home. Agers gestured for them to sit down. A few nods of recognition and Abdullah turned to Ollie who stayed standing.

'Yeah, got some good weed,' said Ollie above the heavy beat.

'Where from?' said Agers. Ollie just shrugged and pulled out a bag, 'two quid a bag.' Agers turned it over.

'You get it from the Somali's?'

'Got my own contacts,' said Ollie feeling important.

'Thought it was their patch round here.'

'A bit of weed won't worry them,' said Ollie his words scratchy as his tongue stuck in a dry mouth.

'They might not think that, but this looks alright. Not much in a bag.'

'Six bags for a tenner,' said Ollie, Agers glanced at one of the others who nodded.

'Alright but I'll give it to you tomorrow, have to get it from the old woman. Sit down and have a smoke,' said Agers.

'Okay,' said Ollie looking around the room and thinking he couldn't argue. 'Can I have a bit of pizza?'

'Sure,' said Agers, passing him a splif. Ollie hesitated. He had enough problems without taking drugs. He took a quick puff and immediately coughed. He handed it on. Perhaps it might help him relax. He reached for a piece of pizza.

'Why you selling, if you don't smoke?' said Agers.

'Need some dough,' said Ollie between bites. He started to delve in his pockets for the little bags.

'Want a beer?'

'No thanks I really need to go,' said Ollie recounting the pile of bags on the carpet.

'Relax man. Breath it gently,' said an older lad who was inhaling from a large joint. A tray with a tub of crushed leaves and papers lay in front of him.

'Gotta go,' said Ollie, 'see you tomorrow.' Abdullah was puffing on a joint but got up and followed him out. At the front door they found a large Mercedes was drawing on to the hard standing.

'Hi boys,' said a middle-aged woman getting out. The car looked very modern. Ollie couldn't help turning and admiring it as they walked away.

'I reckon the way they were smoking the stuff you'll be able to sell them some more in a few days,' said Abdullah.

'Yeah, long as they pay. Was that his Mother?' said Ollie.

'Yes, plenty of money there,' said Abdullah.

'You said you don't smoke?'

'Just being sociable but suppose that's how it starts. I aint going to end up like Nadeem. Phew, but it does get you,' he said rolling his eyes. Powerful stuff. You tried it too.'

'Just a quick cough, not enough to feel anything. Always seems strange putting chemicals in your body you got no control over.' His phone rang. Ollie took it out and stared at it. It was the supplier. For a moment he wanted to ignore it. A sudden tiredness flowing over him as the fear got to him.

'Yes,' he answered as Abdullah walked off.

'Another little run.'

'I can't, not tonight.'

'The only time you can't, is when you're dead. Tomorrow, straight from school. Watch you aint followed.' What was this sudden worry about being followed? Were the police on to them? Fear of being caught stayed with him all the way home.

At home, the flat was empty, with no tempting aroma of dinner. She was late again. He went to his room and slumped on the bed. Emptying his pockets of the unsold bags he slipped them under childhood books and models in the old case under the bed, but he hesitated over the last bag. Perhaps a quick smoke would make him feel better. He deserved a little pleasure and he told himself he was strong enough not to get hooked. On a plate in the kitchen he began to chop the cannabis and rolled it in a page out of an exercise book but then he needed a light. He searched for matches but the flat was all electric. He was still looking and emptying the kitchen cupboards when his mother walked in.

'What are you looking for dear?'

'Nothing,' he said moving sideways to shield the splif which lay on the work surface.

'Nothing?'

'I was hungry.'

'Looking among the utensils?'

'You're late.'

'Trying to earn a little overtime. What were you really after?'

'Nothing! Can't I open a cupboard without getting the third degree,' he said turning. Scooping up the joint, he held it close to his chest, but it was poorly made. Crushed pieces of leaf scattered across the floor. He knelt and started sweeping them together with the palm of his hand.

'What's that? Tobacco?'

'No, it's weed, - happy now?' he said pushing past.

'Oh Ollie, please don't tell me you are taking drugs?' she cried as she followed him to the bedroom. The door slammed in her face. 'Ollie. We have to talk.' She hesitated, then knocked, hesitated again and pushed the door but Ollie was pushing from the other side.

'Leave me alone. It's my room.'

'Alright come out then.'

'Go and make the dinner. That's what you are supposed to do.'

'Ungrateful boy! Your father would be very cross.'

'But he's not here, is he?'

'No, so we have to stick together. I know it's hard, but haven't we done all right till now? Please, please don't mess your future. I'll get dinner now. It's only a packet meal but I have made a proper crumble. Okay?'

'Alright,' muttered Ollie to himself as the pressure on the door eased. Disappointed, yet strangely relieved that he hadn't sampled his stock he wondered what he could tell his Mother. His tale of seeing his friend smoking, when his mother obviously didn't mind, and coming home with a sample amount seemed to satisfy her, especially after she had insisted on seeing the remains of the bag flushed down the sink.

Chapter four. Witness.

Number 47 still had its cigarette ends scattered among the same broken bathroom fittings. Why didn't they clean it up? The door opened before he could knock. Two big lads neither of whom he'd seen before, stood either side, one of whom grabbed Ollie's arm as if to pull him in, but Ollie jerked away. Maggie was shuffling across the floor.

'You're late,' she said as she slumped back into her chair.

'I came straight from school.'

'You see anyone?'

'Nope. No one who looked like the police or anything.'

'The pigs! They're no worry. It's kids, but not from round here.'

'Yeah, you been selling stuff over the road. The Somalis don't like that,' said one of the lads giving Ollie a push. Gold bracelets jangled on the boy's wrist. Where had he heard that voice before?

'You told me to sell it at school.'

'Yeah stupid, but the school's this side, park's the other. Everybody keeps to their territory, everybody happy.'

'None of his business and weed don't count. Another idiot's been supplying snow under their noses.' said Maggie, prodding her phone, 'and they think it's us. Back to Brighton on the Downs run. You remember the place?'

'Yes, I think so,' said Ollie, looking at the two door minders. He had remembered now where he had heard the gold jewellery lad's voice. It had been him who had sent him on his first run and threatened him when he had been robbed. They stared back, nobody said anything. Nothing happened, there was no clock ticking and the room with its closed windows was very quiet, the air heavy with distrust and menace. The woman picked up a novel and the sound of creasing down a new page appeared strangely loud.

Ollie gulped trying to moisten a dry mouth. 'I'll need cash for the ticket.'

'You sold the dope,' snarled gold bracelets.

'Not enough and I need some money - .' but a hand was grabbing him. He twisted away bending low, but the other lad hit him as he did. The blow to his stomach sent him sprawling on the floor, all breath gone. He lay wheezing. His strangulated gasps lost in the scuffle of flying trainers as he was kicked again and again. A hand reached down and hauled him to his feet. Sharp pain ran through him and welled up a fountain of tears. With a final jangle of charms Ollie was tossed effortlessly across the room. Maggie looked up from her book.

'Don't damage him too much; this run's important.'

'Cocky kid, gotta learn.'

Ollie dragged himself to sit leaning against the wall and wiped the tears from his face. As his breath returned and the pain died to a series of manageable aches, he pulled his school bag to him and began to collect its spilled contents. The older man appeared, came over and held a bag out. Ollie pulled himself up the wall wincing. He looked at Maggie. She shrugged, pulled out a wad of notes, peeled off two twenties and flapped them at Ollie. He limped over, took the money and the bag, and went towards the door but he hesitated turning pale. A sob escaped.

'Let him go,' said Maggie. The two toughs stepped back. Still Ollie hesitated, hating their scorn but most of all his own debilitating fear.

'Get you later,' snarled the jewellery collector stepping closer, curling his fist, his face close to the boy's tear-stained cheek. Ollie ran past, jeering laughter following him down the path until the door slammed.

A tall lad he recognised was walking towards him. Ollie remembered how it had been he that had dragged him back to Maggie's. He turned his head to hide his tears.

'They been knocking you about? Is Mo there? He's the one who looks like a Christmas tree.'

'Yeah,' muttered Ollie.

'You travelling? Best keep away from here, someone's going to get it.'

Sitting on the train, he stared down the aisle, blind to passengers or countryside rushing by. He saw only the feet and fists of the youths who had enslaved him, their sneers at his weakness. Even the state of the flop house didn't stir his empathy or indignation. Dozing on return was a relief until he awoke sweaty from a muddled nightmare. He shivered in the cold carriage.

Emerging from Earlsfield station, he found the dark evening was made more depressing by the steady rain. The car's headlights and streetlamps reflected off the wet streets, making the hidden corners and in-between spaces even blacker and more threatening. He glanced around, apprehension replacing the zombie like tiredness. Stepping out he stumbled to a faster pace. He'd only done the length of one street when at a corner he heard a shout. Glancing down the side street he saw a group of youths chasing another towards him. Lamp light reflected off the fugitive's gold necklace and staring eyes.

Turning around to run, Ollie collided with another youth. A knife clattered on to the pavement; a hunting knife with a bone handle, not a kitchen knife. For a moment they stared at it and then at each other. Then Ollie was bowled over by a second lad who was also running to cut off their quarry. Ollie scrambled to the side of the pavement. Easing himself up, he stared at the scene. Forever etched in his memory, he saw as if in slow motion, the repeated thrusts of the knife, the crowd like some wild wolf pack surrounding and pulling down their prey. Each second carefully recorded in his brain. But then time changed and in an instant they were scattering, leaving a writhing figure on the wet tarmac. Each went the way they had come. The one with the knife passing close to Ollie who jumped back to the fence expecting to be the next victim, but the snarling expression and gesture were enough to say Ollie would never tell.

He continued to stare. He had to run but his legs couldn't move, he ought to help, but fear wouldn't let him. The police sirens bought relief, and he took a step away. Doors were slamming, adults were everywhere.

'He's one of them,' shouted a woman pointing. He awoke and ran; a flying run and he didn't stop until his key was jamming in the flat door. He burst in and sank on to the settee. His mother, shocked out of a TV watching stupor, sat up.

'What on ea -.'

'Sorry, need the loo,' said Ollie, jumping up again and rushing to relieve himself. When he returned to the room she was standing, hands on hips, waiting.

'There was a knifing; police everywhere. I just ran,' he said looking at his feet.

'Are you alright?' she said.

'Yeah, suppose so.'

'You don't look it,' she said coming over and bending to look at his face. 'Did you actually see it?'

'Sort of.'

'Did you recognise any of them?'

'No, I just ran,' he lied.

'You got to stop staying out; come straight home from school. It's too dangerous. Was he hurt bad?'

'I dunno really,' he said sinking down on the sofa.

'You've got to keep away from evil men like that?'

'Oh Mum, it isn't like that. It was -' but as he saw again what it was like, his words died.

'You going to tell the police what you saw?'

'No, definitely not,' he said rising and going to his room, 'no way.'

In the morning he arrived late at the school gates, his face drawn and pale, but Abdullah was waiting for him.

'You're late and you look like death,' said Abdullah.

'Yeah well.'

'Did you hear there was a stabbing down by the station?' said Abdullah.

'It wasn't by -.' He started to say then looked away.

'Hey what do you know about it? Bet it was one of your gang.'

'I'm not in any gang, but look, Abdullah, if you tell anyone, I'll be dead meat, but I saw it all.'

'You were part of it then?'

'I've not sunk that low, just happened to be there. It was horrific and the guy who got it was one of those who gave me the deliveries. Hunted down like some animal.'

'Then you are part of the same side,' said Abdullah turning into the school gates, Ollie sloping along behind him. Everyone else had gone into class so the corridors were empty.

'It aint like that, I'm just a courier. Did he die?'

'According to my old man's newspaper he's critical.'

'Look, my mum wants me to check up on my sister after school. Can you come, just in case he's there?'

'Who's he?'

'Her nasty boyfriend, Todd.'

'I thought my family was bad, but yeah I'll come, you need a full-time minder.'

'Thanks, and what's our excuse for being late?'

'Easy, when you look as ill as you do.'

Todd's house was mid-terrace Victorian with the front door three feet from the pavement. Abdullah hovered in the road, clearly not anxious to be part of any family scene. Ollie knocked and when nothing happened after two minutes, knocked again. The door jerked open.

'Yeah wha'd you want?' snarled Todd.

'Just eh, wanted to see my sister.'

'She aint here, so clear off.'

'Where is she then?' said Ollie stepping back slightly.

'Out, down the shop.'

'Then she won't be long. I'll come in and wait, shall I?' said Ollie, wondering at his own audacity

'You can stay out here for all I care.' The door slammed. Ollie sat on the short wall that left just enough gap between the pavement and house for the bins. Abdullah joined him.

'I'd not be much good as a minder if he decided to knock you around. He must work out a lot.' They continued to sit and watch the traffic and passers-by. 'Can't stay here for ever, I got homework to do.'

'The shop's only just down the road.'

'If that's where she went.' After another twenty minutes Abdullah stood up. 'See you tomorrow.'

'Hang on, here she is,' said Ollie, 'Sasha, you alright?'

'Yeah,' she said, glancing at Abdullah, and then with head down knocked at the door.

'Been shopping?' said Abdullah.

'Eh?'

'Shopping, where's the shopping?' said Abdullah.

'Dunno what you on a'bout,' said Sasha. The door swung open and she stepped straight in. Ollie moved quickly. Todd tried to grab him and close the door at the same time, but he slid through. Inside the house was clean, apart from a scattering of shoes in the entrance and an unfinished meal on the table. The two white leather settees looked and smelt quality.

'I told you to scat,' said Todd.

'I just want a word, that's all,' said Ollie walking through to the kitchen. He stood fidgeting, picked up a spoon for no reason and put it down again. Why wasn't she coming? He heard whispers.

'You must go. Todd can get very rough when he wants,' said Sasha coming in.

'Yeah, but Mums worried. You need to get out. He aint no good,' whispered Ollie.

'Can't, he's my man.'

'Please Sasha,' he said closing the door. 'If I get you some cash, you could join Julie in Spain. Get a job there.'

'Spain. Why would I want to go to frigging Spain?'

'Just to get away.'

'Leave it Ollie, I'm alright.'

'You don't look it and what's that yellow mark on your neck?'

'Eh nothing; I walked into a door. Just tell Mum I'm OK.'

'But you aren't. He said you were shopping. What's he got you to do? You can't just sit round here all day.'

'Nothing.'

'Are you delivering coke?'

With a crash the kitchen door swung open, slamming against the work surface.

'I told you to shove off,' said Todd, standing legs wide in classic shooting stance, a small automatic pistol, held in both hands pointing at Ollie.

'Pshaw, pshaw,' he said and then laughing, put the gun up and blew away imaginary smoke from its barrel.

'He's just going,' said Sasha, but Ollie was frozen to the spot. He licked his lips, felt his insides were going to fall out, and finally stumbled for the door.

'Browning 32,' said Todd, holding the pistol in his open palm so it could be admired and even in his fear Ollie was curious enough to look. The blue steel of the weapon with its checker plate butt was fascinating, the ultimate deadly tool. Its horrible beauty was slightly marred by the way someone had crudely ground the serial number off the side. Todd closed his fist, to again point the gun at Ollie's head. 'Wouldn't want it to go off, would we?' Ollie nearly fell through the front door in his haste. He heard laughing before the door slammed.

Abdullah went to catch Ollie, but he steadied himself and then lurched to sit on the wall.'

'He belt you?'

'No, just pointed a gun at my head.'

'Hell, and you wanted me to back you up? Let's get out of here,' said Abdullah pulling at Ollie's sleeve. With a last backward glance at the house, they walked briskly away.

The following evening Ollie was trying to concentrate on a difficult English essay when his phone rang. It was Abdullah.

'Have you heard bro. Been a drive by and somebody dead. One of the Somalis' my brother reckons. Keep your head down, its war out there. See you tomorrow.'

Chapter Five. Hospital

On the way to school, they were passed by several police cars, sirens wailing but although the news and rumours were on everybody's lips Ollie received no calls. No instant demand to catch a train, no threats, no risk of prison or stabbing. Perhaps his involvement was over. He could just get on with trying to educate himself to something better. Sasha would have to sort her own life. Yet he couldn't forget her gaunt face. Two days later at school it was a different type of message. The constant bleeps of texts received during an unusually quiet lesson, mid-afternoon, forced him to look. It was his mother.

'Sasha in hospital, I'm there, A&E. Don't worry, Mum.' He stared at the text. Despair flooded over him.

'Well, I'll take that,' said his teacher all six foot of him glaring down.

'Please, it's my mum. My sister's in hospital; look.'

'Huh, likely tale,' the teacher said, hand outstretched for the phone.

Ollie looked at the man and just shook his head and started gathering his books.

'Sorry sir.' Ollie said with a sob. Standing he pushed passed. No one stopped him or said anything as, with bag over his shoulder and clenched fists, he left. At the hospital he found his mother in the crowded waiting room with red eyes and tissue in one hand.

'What's happened? Is she alright?' he blurted out.

'She's been beaten up. A neighbour called an ambulance - she was so pretty.'

'Won't they let you see her?' Ollie said after a moment but under his breath. 'I'll kill him.'

'They say I can in a moment. Think they are x-raying her.'

'I'll get you a cup of tea.'

It was half an hour before they were allowed through. A doctor who looked about nineteen was very carefully stitching her chin.

'Don't move,' he commanded as she looked up. 'We don't want to spoil my best needlework.'

Ollie put his arm round his mother as they looked down on Sasha's swollen face. 'The scan didn't show any internal bleeding but there are three cracked ribs and her wrist is broken.'

They stood watching the doctor's painstaking work. Her Mum shuffled around and pulled a chair over to sit beside her.

'Right, that's finished. She will be sent up to theatre to have a pin put into her wrist later, but the police will want to talk to her first,' said the doctor pulling the curtains around.

'I'll kill the bastard,' said Ollie as soon as he had left.

'You're fourteen, a child. It's for the police to sort out. Have you spoken to them, Sasha?'

'I can't,' she said and winced, 'Ouch.'

'They will need to charge him,' said Mrs Lansbury as Ollie coughed. A uniformed policeman was hovering at the gap in the curtains.

'We need every detail,' he said drawing another chair over. 'Please, I know it must hurt but the sooner we get the facts down, the quicker we can apprehend your attacker.' Sasha tried to look away but just moaned.

'Your full name?'

As the officer took down the background information, Ollie thought, at least now the family would be together again, with Todd out of their lives but would he come after her if she gave evidence? The thought of him seeking to silence them made him shiver. His thoughts were interrupted when he heard Sasha say she didn't know her attacker.

'He must have been a burglar,' she said.

'Oh yeah. It was Todd, her boyfriend, he's a drug dealer,' exclaimed Ollie.

'Were you there?' said the policeman turning to Ollie.

'No, but he's done it many times before. Sasha's scared. We need protection.'

'So, what's this Todd's surname?'

'Osbourne, but it wasn't him,' said Sasha with a little sob.

'We'll keep you safe,' said Ollie, but he knew it wasn't true. Perhaps she was right, and it was safer not doing anything.

'He's hit you before?' said the policeman his pen and notebook poised.

'No! I'm not saying anything.'

'If you women don't tell the truth, these men carry on with their beatings. It's only when people have the guts to be a witness that we can put them where they belong. We can keep you safe.'

'Yeah sure! It was a burglar, alright?' said Sasha.

'We can still arrest him and call you as a witness. He mustn't get away with it.'

'No comment.'

'Well, think about it,' he sighed. 'And your family might help you to understand it's your duty. Now you son, tell me about the drugs.'

'No comment,' said Ollie looking at his shoes.

'I've plenty to do without wasting time on those who don't care. We must all stop the drugs and stabbings. Contact me when you see sense.'

After he had left, they sat in silence until Mrs Lanesbury went off to the toilet.

'Quick Sasha, tell me why he hurt you so badly; before Mum comes back.'

'Can't.'

'You've got to. I won't grass on you or him. I just need to understand, cos I'm sort of mixed up with his crowd too. Next time I see him, will he be out to get me, or will I be trying to kill him? Gotta know how the land lies.'

'Ollie, don't you have anything to do with drugs, the pushers keep killing each other. You'd break Mum's heart if you get in with the wrong crowd,' she said grimacing as she moved.

'You didn't think of that when you shacked up with Todd.'

'No, well I've paid for it now, haven't I.'

'You're not going back are you?'

'No - but it wasn't his fault, I did something stupid.'

'What was so stupid that he had to smash up your face?'

'Nothing.'

'Come on Sasha, please, before Mum returns.'

'You know his little plaything. You saw it. I was supposed to take it back, but they were doing stop and search. I panicked and dropped it from the bridge.'

'It was him! The shooting; he's a murderer?'

'Now you see why I can't grass on him. He'd kill me.'

'Shush, here's Mum.'

'You'd better go Ollie, if you've homework to do,' said Mrs Lanesbury.

'I can stay longer if you want.'

'No, I'm alright until the x-ray. You go. Have a look through the freezer for something to eat, I'll eat here.'

'Okay, bye Sasha,' he said turning to find his way out through the various mini wards of A & E. Deep in thought he nearly walked into a doctor and then realised he was getting lost. He retraced his steps. Outside he went to dial Abdullah but before he could, it rang.

'Need you at Maggie's tonight,' said an unrecognised voice.

'But my sisters in hospital.'

'Yeah, and you'll join her if you aren't sharpish.' With head down Ollie walked on.

An hour later he was knocking on the door of no 47. He quickly stepped inside ready to dodge any blows in his direction but beyond the one teenager who opened the door, the room was empty.

'Maggie,' shouted the lad.

'Alright, I'm coming,' she shouted from another room before wobbling in, Todd following behind.

'It's you is it? Easy run. You sold them wraps for your travelling money?'

'No and I was promised £300 a run too,' said Ollie, moving warily to the middle of the room furthest from the two men. Was he really going to ask them to start paying? His insides were turning to water but if he didn't stick up for himself, he was lost.

'You owe for the stolen stuff,' said Maggie.

'But that was a set up,' said Ollie. The room went very quiet, the silence settling into a deep chill. Finally, Maggie moved in her chair. Todd stepped around her. Ollie backed closer to the door, but the other lad stepped in front of it.

'You disrespect us, you're dead,' said Todd.

'But it's true, isn't it,' said Ollie but it came out as a squeak.

'You wanna end up like your sister?' Ollie just stared, his hands curling into fists. He knew Todd could cripple him, but his hatred was stronger than his fear. Todd stared back and then moved his right hand, positioning for a back handed slap.

'What's this about,' said Maggie.

'My woman, the stupid bitch ditched the tool.'

'What's it to him?'

'She's his sister.'

'Don't mark him,' said Maggie,' 'Here's another forty for the ticket. Can you remember two addresses,' she added turning to Ollie after glaring at Todd. With two parcels in his bag, he left but Todd followed him outside. Glancing over his shoulder Ollie went to run.

'I ain't going to hurt you. How's Sasha?' called Todd.

'What you care? You put her there.'

'She messed up, needed a lesson that's all.'

It was a complicated journey on slow trains, dropping off first in Sevenoaks and then Tonbridge. The second contact was in a smart pub where Ollie felt very conspicuous in his school uniform. The place was busy, and he had to wait for his contact, the ginger haired barman to be free.

'You Kevin?' asked Ollie.

'Of course, that's me,' said the barman in what Ollie thought was a posh accent.

'Are you expecting a delivery,' said Ollie looking around. Somehow the bistro pub with its well-heeled customers didn't look like the usual place for addicts.

'Actually, it was promised last night,' said the barman his hand held out.' A middle-aged gent in a blue pinstriped suit and yellow tie pushed to the bar beside Ollie.

'G & T old boy and a chardonnay please.'

'In a moment, sir,' said the barman his hand still extended. 'Just hand over the rock please. It's been paid for.'

Ollie passed over the parcel, took a last glance around and left as the barman put the package under the counter and went back to serving drinks.

At school the following day he couldn't concentrate. He didn't get into trouble for his poor attention span but there was a general air of "teacher disappointment." Ollie was one of a small group that gave the staff hope that their hard work might not be totally wasted. A hope that was leaking away. As he was leaving school, the phone rang; Sasha's number.

'Need you at no 47,' said a male voice. The speaker rang off before Ollie could decide who it was.

When he arrived, the tall youth that Ollie had met before, let him in. Todd was pacing the floor. Maggie's chair was empty.

'Right,' said Todd, 'You take the phone and this stuff. Three for £35 single £15. You got a bike? It's all counted, be back here at eleven with the cash.'

'What?' said Ollie, staring at the phone being held out to him.

'Punters ring you, tell you what they want. You deliver; simple. Baz here, takes over later. Need a different face.'

Ollie took the package and put it in his bag. He left, holding the phone like it might bite. He had just arrived home when he had the first call.

'You got some boggies?' said the caller.

'Yeah, three for £35.'

'Bring them round then,' said the caller giving an address. Closing the door, Ollie quickly pulled out an exercise book and pen from his bag and wrote it down.

'Who was on the phone?' said his mother coming into the hall.

'Nobody you know. I'm starving.'

'Well its ready as you're late.'

'Sorry,' he said throwing his bag in the corner. 'Did you see Sasha?'

'Yes, and she's coming home tomorrow, I need you to clear any of your stuff out of the box room tonight.'

'Ok,' he said, 'I need to get my bike out anyway.'

He was only half-way through his shepherd's pie when he received his second call. He scrambled on the floor, grabbed the book and wrote down the new address. Bringing it back to the table he avoided his mother's eyes. He knew neither road. By the time he'd hastily eaten some cake and pumped the tyres up on his bike he had received another two orders. He found an old A to Z and sitting on the hall floor tried to work out a circular route.

'Going to tell me what's going on?' said his mother coming in.

'Covering for a friend who does the Just Eats deliveries. I need to go,' he said pushing past.

'Ollie, don't lie.'

With head down he pushed the bike though the doorway. Hating his mother, yet at the same time wanting to turn and be hugged by her like she did when he was five.

'Ollie!' But his feet were echoing down the corridor. Outside, he set the navigator on the phone. He had no holder so had it to hold it, as well as grip the handlebars. He wobbled out into the night. Most of the addresses were close together but varied from multi-million-pound penthouse flats to sordid flop houses. Over cycle lanes, along pavements and life-risking busy roads. Hugging the road edge as busy traffic streamed by, he was concentrating on his route when a car slowed down beside him.

'Where're your lights?' yelled the uniformed policeman from his patrol car. Ollie wobbled and slid to a stop.

'Get some, before you get squashed.' The car moved on leaving a shaken Ollie. By the end of the evening not only was he having to worry about the security of the bike when he left it in the street, but also the £400 cash he was carrying. He was also on the lookout for any-one else who might be from a gang. He didn't even know whose patch he was on. He was back at number 47 by 10.45pm.

'You're early.' said Maggie. 'You done all the deliveries you got?'

'Yes, and I'm too tired to do any more,' he said, emptying the bag on to a side table and handing her the cash.

'You don't come back until it's all sold, or your shift's done and be careful with them little bags. Don't need any to split. Baz,' she shouted and then started tallying the money, flick edge counting, as quick as any bank cashier. 'Four hundred and five pounds. What's he got left?' she added to Baz as he came down the stairs.

'Sixteen,' hc said, after he had laid them out neatly.

'Should be right, I sold two singles at £15 and eleven threes,' said Ollie. Were they trying to cheat him again?

Maggie counted on her fingers.

'Yeah that's right,' she finally said. Ollie with a nervous glance at Baz, stepped closer and held out his hand.

'Please.'

'Todd said I weren't to give you any cos of what your sister done,' said Maggie.

'You knew he beat her up horribly?'

'She had it coming.'

'Is Todd in charge?'

'You ask too many questions. Disrespect Todd, and you're history.'

Ollie gulped but his hand remained out.

'Get out of here,' she said handing him two twenty-pound notes.

Back at the flat he tried to enter as quietly as possible. His mother was always in bed by eleven. The handlebars bumped on the door, but the hall light was on anyway. She was sitting on a dining room chair in the hall.

'Well, you going to tell me what you are up to?'

'I said I was delivering for a friend. Forty pounds. Do you want some for housekeeping?'

'Mm, you keep it. Your schoolwork's more important than a few pounds.' Pushing past he went to his room. He just needed to collapse on his bed and sleep but all he could do was sit and stare at the wall. He couldn't carry on like this. He awoke in the morning to find he had slept in his uniform. At breakfast, heavy with sleep, he felt a mess, and could only grunt replies to his mother, before she rushed off to work. He tried to concentrate at school and at a few minutes before home-time turned his phone off.

Walking home with Abdullah, he saw four youths on the other side of the road watching them. Stepping off the pavement they approached. Abdullah turned to run.

'It's okay, I think. I know one of them,' said Ollie recognising Baz.

'That doesn't make em safe,' said Abdullah walking back the way they had come.

'Hi bros,' said Baz, 'We recon you need to meet some of the gang.

'Yeah, hello then,' said Ollie.

'You collect from Maggie. You work for us. You mess with her you mess with us, who's your mate?' said Baz giving Ollie a hi-five.

'I aint nothing to do with this,' said Abdullah, edging further away.

'You either a bro or you the enemy,' said one of the others. He was very dark skinned and heavily built.

'Just a friend,' said Abdullah continuing to walk. He stopped far enough away to be able to watch yet with a good start if he had to run.

'All local stuff goes through us.'

'And Todd?'

'He's with us. He does a bit of his own, but we all share.' There were more hi-fives and then the four slouched off.

'Widening your friendship group, are you?' said Abdullah catching up with Ollie.

'Better on our side than against,' said Ollie.

'Possibly? Possibly not.'

Back at the flat, it appeared empty with no lights on. No Sasha crashing around the place. He found his mother in the corner of the lounge.

'Where's Sasha?' said Ollie.

'That bastard picked her up from the hospital,' she sobbed.

'But why did she go with him?'

'Dunno, all she did was send me a text, "sorry he needs me, I'm forgiven.

'What, after all he did!'

'Yeah, women can be pretty stupid over men sometimes,'

He didn't sleep that well and kept his phone off most of the day, telling Abdullah that if he needed him, he would have to come around. In the evening he couldn't concentrate. He hurried out. When he reached Todd's home, he hovered, not daring to knock. Walking away he stopped at a house that was part of the terrace opposite. It had a "for rent" sign and was obviously empty. Sitting in the open porch he could see the door of Todd's house. It was ideal, hardly any of the passers-by saw him, and those that did, ignored him. However, neither Sasha nor Todd appeared. Eventually at eleven pm he wandered home.

The following night, after having dumped his bag at home he went straight out. He had just settled down in the porch when Todd emerged to stand looking up and down the street. Ollie stopped breathing, for what seemed like ages as Todd appeared to look through him but then he turned on his heel and walked briskly away. He didn't take the car.

Ollie breathed out. He hadn't been seen! His intention had been to visit Sasha when Todd was absent, but he suddenly changed his mind. The more he knew about Todd's activities the better. He started to follow at a safe distance. The evening was overcast and consequentially it was dark between streetlamps.

At first Ollie thought his quarry was going to No 47 but instead he turned towards the park. Staying back, Ollie continued to shadow him. On the outskirts of the park, he watched as a group of lads began to collect around Todd. Then Baz rode up on a bike and handed Todd a package. The package was split, and money was quickly changing hands as Baz peddled away. It was then that Ollie noticed a lad leaning against a tree watching him. He backed away and as he turned a corner, he broke into a run. Had he been recognised? Back at Sasha's house, Ollie knocked, the urgent banging of, "hurry up, I haven't much time." Sasha cautiously opened the door.

'You shouldn't be here,' she whispered, her eyes flicking up and down the road.

'Just let me in. Why the heck did you come back?' he said, pushing past. Sasha followed him into the kitchen. It was bright and modern.

'If Todd finds you here, he'll go mad.'

'You were supposed to stay with us, like safe. Sasha, you are still beautiful and intelligent. You could get a decent job and live at home. I could sleep in the box room,' he said trying not to look at the black bruises that covered neck and face and the red weal of her stitched chin.

'You don't know him; he isn't always violent. He can be quite loving.'

'Oh yeah. Even if he's a saint 50% of the time, during the other 50% he's the devil. He killed someone, remember?'

'I love him. I can help him, change him.'

'No, you can't, and how come your phones being used for crack sales?'

'Even if I came home, he'd just come and grab me.'

'But you can get the police to get some sort of order to stop him.'

'He wouldn't take no notice.'

'But then he'd get arrested and you'd be free.'

'For how long? When he came out, he'd be even more dangerous.'

'We can protect you.'

'You? what can you do?' she laughed. 'Ollie, you're a skinny kid. One blow from him and you'd be in hospital for a month.'

'It's good to see you laugh,' said Ollie but then they both froze as there was a rattle at the front door. 'Can I get out the back?'

'It's just a little yard,' she whispered fear etching her face. Ollie slid the bolt back and carefully opened the door.

'Where are yer?' shouted Todd as a door slammed. 'Need you to drop off some snow.'

Ollie gently closed the back door and looked around. A high back wall separated it from another line of terraced houses. To one side a very high fence, the other side an equally high wall. No way out. He banged into a garden chair. The grating sound was quite loud in the confined space. Two shrubs in pots, a rusty BBQ and the chairs, no shed or trees. Nothing to hide behind. He had to get out and quick. He shuffled from one foot to another his eyes swivelling from one high wall to another.

'Gotta climb it,' he muttered but running at the side wall wouldn't give enough speed to scramble to the top. The wall was Victorian yellow brick, the pointing soft and worn away. Could he dig his finger between the bricks? Would his trainers get enough grip? With a last look at the house door, he stretched up and started to climb.

Every finger end hurt as his nails gripped the brick edges. Dragging himself up he sought to dig his trainers into the little gaps between the bricks. One stayed put, the other slipped out. He hung, foot scraping the bricks desperately trying to get some grip. Pain from hanging by his finger ends cramped his hands. Another step up, more scuffing on the wall with his feet. One more reach, expecting any moment to fall. Finally, he reached the top and dragged himself over to lie on his stomach, easing the pain in his fingers. It was too high to jump so he turned to climb back down. Glancing back, he saw someone standing at the back door watching him. Todd leant down and picked up a flowerpot shaking out the half dead plant.

Ollie slid down, feet scrabbling to find a mortar gap wide enough to support him. The flowerpot crashed against the top of the wall, showering him with ceramic splinters. Half-way down both feet slipped so he thrust away, to fall heavily on the paving. He limped to a seat. He didn't want to look at his fingers but inspecting them, he saw that while scuffed red they weren't as damaged as he expected. Several nails were broken, and they were all jammed with brick dust.

Looking up, he saw that this house had the same walls either side, with no easy exit. The house looked empty with no one at home. He sighed but this time used an upturned flowerpot on top of a table as a starting point for his climb. It wobbled badly but sliding down into the third garden a voice rang out.

'Hey you. What you doing? I'm ringing the police,' said an elderly man stepping into the yard from his doorway. He waved his walking stick.

'Sorry, I'm not a burglar. My sister's boyfriend just came home. She lives two doors up and he threatened to beat me up.'

'Is he the black guy built like a tank?'

'That's him.'

'I see, do you want to come through the house?'

'Thanks, I'm not sure I can scale any more of these walls,' said Ollie looking at his nails again.

'They're bleeding, you need to get something on them,' said the man leading Ollie through the house. Ollie had to walk round piles of clutter, magazines, and two bikes.

'Do you want a cup of tea?'

'No, but thanks for letting me out. If my sister ever starts screaming can you ring the police.'

'Not much good asking me, I don't hear so well.'

The following day when he came out of school, he saw Baz sitting on his bike leaning against a wall smoking. Seeing Ollie, he flicked his cigarette into the gutter and rode over. Ollie looked around, fearing an ambush. Abdullah had already left. Ollie felt very vulnerable even as other children pushed past.

'Hi,' said Baz, giving Ollie a high five. 'Got a county run for you.'

'What about Todd? I need to avoid him.'

'Hell, that's difficult. You'd better not come in. Meet you in the street, end of the road. Maggie says she'll pay you. Reckons you've been there before.'

'I'll be there at six then, end of the road. Make sure she sends out some cash.'

A quick meal with more excuses for his mum. She didn't say anything just nodded, looking sad. Didn't she believe anything he said anymore? Had she finally given up on him?

He was very careful when he approached Maggie's neighbourhood. Even after he had seen Baz, he was poised to run. Baz waved and went inside. Ollie waited, nervously, shifting from one leg to another, trying to decide which road would give him the clearest escape. The grey-haired Nigerian appeared from a small block of flats further up the road, one hand tucked inside his jacket obviously holding a package. Looking around nervously, he went into number 47. A few minutes later Baz emerged.

'Right it's Downs, you know Brighton, your route. Here's some cash. £60,' said Baz. Ollie sighed. Not the sort of money he ought to be paid.

'Worth more than that,' he said but at least he would have some change from the fare. The trip went to the usual place. The only good thing was he found a Country Life magazine on the train to read. It was full of posh properties in Devon, a different world.

Chapter six. Arrest.

Leaving school, the following day, he saw that Baz was again waiting for him.

'I can't do these runs every night, it's exhausting,' said Ollie as Baz cycled over.

'Just local,' said Baz, handing him a phone. He glanced at the stream of children pushing past. 'Thirty wraps, same price, you'll need a bike,' he added, handing over a rolled-up plastic bag. Abdullah walked past, shook his head and carried on walking.

'Alright but I can't cope with any more this week.'

The first phone call came in as soon as he reached home. Making excuses about dinner he ate a slice of bread and jam and cycled out. He had done three deliveries, with two to go when it rang again. One more customer.

'Have you got some rock candy; crack?'

'Yup, three for £35, okay?'

'Yeah, when can you deliver to Martland Street?'

'About forty minutes, two more drop offs before then.'

'Great, flat fourteen, Chestnut Apartments, we'll have the cash. Post c -.'

'I know the road.' It was nearer to an hour before he got there as one of the customers had argued about paying. The flat was on the third floor with no lift. Typical ex-council. Already another two orders had come in. He clattered up the stairs, breathing heavily by the time he was ringing the bell. A man in his twenties, dressed in holed jeans and scruffy leather jacket opened the door.

'Come in,' he said standing back from the door. 'Do you want a drink?'

'Eh, no thanks,' said Ollie glancing past, 'just the cash.'

'Yeah of course but I don't want to talk here, do I? I'm quite safe.'

'Three for thirty-five pounds,' whispered Ollie, his hand held out. The door in the flat behind, opened slightly but no one came out.

'It's proper rock candy, crack?' said the man.

'Yes.'

'You know it's crack?'

'Do you want it or not? I'm behind with my deliveries.' Was the man stupid or was he going to try to rob him? He backed away from the door and glanced at the door behind him, ready to leap down the stairs.

'Hey, it's alright, don't worry, here's your money,' said the man, holding out some crisp new notes. Ollie breathed out, snatched the money, and counted out three small bags into the man's outstretched palm. The door behind him flew open.

'Got yer.' Ollie was grabbed by strong hands.

'I must warn you - .' began the policeman as he started to recite Ollie's legal rights.

'He's only a kid,' said another policeman, who joined them.

'Let go,' muttered Ollie but that was all he managed to say as they bundled him down the stairs.

'When you are in the car, we can ring a parent,' said the first policeman.

'My bike,' said Ollie at the bottom, pointing to where it was tucked under the stairs. 'Please.'

'Shouldn't be selling drugs.'

'But it'll get stolen,'

'Tough.'

'In the car the silence hung in layers. The cold shock of "it's finally happened, you're really in it now," layer. The, what would everybody think, the pain for his mother, and the layer of his own incompetence. He wanted to lash out, to hate them all, those that had made his world, governments, schools, his father for not being there, himself, but especially the drug dealers. Yet he also wanted to slink away and curl up in a corner and never have to face problems again.

At the station he sat in a small office with his head in his hands. Officers were going in and out and a female officer was working at a computer but also watching him closely. He finally looked up, the shock gradually dissipating. Perhaps the arrest would at least mean they wouldn't make him do any more deliveries. To be out of it would be a relief. There was nothing he could do for Sasha now. All hope for her gone.

He wasn't looking forward to being questioned. If he grassed on Maggie, he was dead meat. Every kid on the street would be out to get him. How had he become so involved? The self-accusations continued to crunch up his insides. Worries that the police would tie him up in slick questions, trick him into revealing too much, began to grow.

He tried in his head to rehearse answers to unknown questions. He knew he had to overcome his fears and his worries about his mother, but he couldn't shake off the grip of despair. Somehow, he had to rescue the situation. By some means he had to make it right with her. Ideas began to come, wild ideas of escape, crazy thoughts of revenge. When she arrived, they took him into an interview room, but he was still thinking hard.

'Right,' said a plain clothes policeman, turning on a professional looking recording machine and giving the date, time and names of all present. 'Ollie Lanesbury, you are being questioned about supplying class A drugs. This is a very serious offense. You were found to be carrying nine packets of crack cocaine.' He nodded to the little pile of bags and small stack of money on a side table. 'Where did it come from?'

'Shouldn't he have a solicitor?' sobbed his mum.

The detective and uniformed female officer looked at each other. 'Of course, if he wants one. He was caught red handed dealing crack. We just need to know where he got it from. It's a very serious offense. He's looking at three years in a youth prison. If he tells us where it came from it might help,' said the female officer.

'Look boy you're really going down,' said the detective leaning over the table jarring the tape recorder. Flecks of spit landed on the surface. 'Not nice those places, full of nasty kids.'

'I can't,' said Ollie looking at the floor.

'Haven't you any thought for your mum?' said the female officer.

'You'll tell us eventually. You're just wasting time,' said the detective,

'I want to talk in private to D.S. Rawlins,' said Ollie.

'You what?'

'I want to talk to him and only him,' said Ollie looking up, and eye to eye.

'What's he got to do with a little squirt like you?'

'Just get him.'

'This isn't his case. He has enough to do,' said the female officer.

'I'll wait.'

'You'll be kept in.'

'So, but if we have a chat it might help.'

'Why do you want to waste his time?'

'Will you give him bail,' said Mrs. Lanesbury.

'Not until he's told us where he obtained the crack; he could be in danger,' said the detective.

'I am in danger. Mum's in danger. All of us, so you'd better hurry up and get him.' The female officer exchanged a look with the detective.

'Oh, alright I'll see if he's in. He aint going to be pleased, pausing the tape at 20.20,' said the detective standing.

'You won't be able to see him in private,' said the female officer after he had gone.

'I can talk to him in the corridor, can't I?'

'Not unless I'm present,' said the female officer.

'Out of earshot, that's fine.'

'Ollie why are you making more trouble? What's this policeman to you?' said his mother.

'You wait, it'll be okay.'

When Rawlins arrived, he didn't look happy. He scowled and stared at Ollie and then recognition.

'You're in big trouble,' he said.

'I know but I need to talk to you outside.'

'It won't make any difference. Just tell them everything you know, and they'll do their best.'

'No, give me two minutes. I reckon you won't regret it,' said Ollie standing and stepping towards the door. The female officer stretched an arm out to contain him.

'Alright two minutes,' said Rawlins. Ollie followed him outside and stopped at the end of the corridor with the female officer standing at the other end.

'I know where the gun is, the one they used in the drive-by shooting,' Ollie whispered. 'I was witness to the stabbing of the boy the day before. But I need total protection, for me, my mum and especially my sister. Guaranteed in writing, no charges and no record.'

'Oh yeah, you were involved in both of those crimes?'

'No, I wasn't but I still know. I can identify the knife and at least one of the lads who did it. I'm willing to stand up in court, but I need a new life away from London. Somewhere like Exeter. Yes Exeter.'

'You've been reading too many American novels. It doesn't work like that here and why should I believe you?'

'It was a Browning 32; I saw it and can identify it because something had been ground off the butt.'

'Hell, you've have been busy.'

'You wanted to know about the gangs, how it all works. I can give you everything. All of them. Up to you,' said Ollie, looking the detective in the eye. He folded his arms. A confident gesture but it was to stop the shaking of his hands. Pointing to the female officer he added, 'I'll go and sit down. She can get us tea and sandwiches while you think it out or get clearance or whatever you must do? I want it in writing and I'm hungry.'

'Alright Ollie, if you are telling the truth you'll get what you want,' said D.S. Rawlins with a smile.

'Thanks. I'm risking my life here so I'm trusting you.'

'You can but you still want it in writing?'

'Headed notepaper signed by you will do. But you need to release me quick. If they hear I've been picked up by you, the chance to nab them actually holding the stuff will be lost.'

'What crimes have you personally been involved in?'

'Just delivering.'

'County lines?'

'Yeah, got trapped by them.'

'Okay Wrainwright, get the boy and his mother something decent to eat. I'll be back in a moment.'

'But sergeant that will leave him unguarded.'

'Don't worry, he's not going to do a runner. He needs us as much as we need him. I'll have a cheese sandwich and white coffee.'

The scrappy piece of paper didn't say much but Ollie was happy with it and secreted it away in his most innermost pocket.

'The gun is in the Wandle river under the footbridge off Steerforth road. My sister threw it away when she was taking it back to the bloke who hires them out. Her partner Todd was the shooter. She's very vulnerable but she knows a lot about it all and can be a witness. She's the most important one to protect, but first, if you want to hit the suppliers you need to let me go with the rock candy and cash. The distribution point is number 47 South Street, but the drugs are never held there but in one of the flats opposite. The block is number 68, I don't know which flat, as there are six in the building, numbered A to F.

What you need is to wait till I get a call to do a run. Then you can have one man following me, someone who looks the least like a copper. I go to the house and a few minutes later an old guy, a Nigerian who seems to have faded a bit, like he hasn't seen the sun for twenty years, with grey frizzy hair will come out of the flat and bring the stuff over. As soon as he leaves, you follow the old geezer back to the right flat and then quickly raid 47 before I leave.' Ollie looked at his audience expecting a question, but they just stared. The female officer's mouth was open. He took a sip of tea and a couple of bites of his sandwich.

'Then I'll slink away, you pick me up and then collect Todd from his house before he starts killing anyone; alright?' said Ollie looking around at his stunned audience. 'Come on, I have to get this stuff back before they twig,' he said standing. He stuffed in the last piece of sandwich.

'Is all this true?' said his mum and then, turning to the police, 'You can't let him do this, can you? Go into danger like that?'

'Get the drugs and cash,' said Rawlins ignoring Mrs Lanesbury. 'I'll use my own car.'

'The chief won't like it. You can't just give him the stuff back,' said the female officer.

'No Ollie I can't really involve you, and I can't let you take the crack,' said Rawlins.

Ollie's phone rang. Without a second glance at the police, he reached across the table and picked it up. 'Yeah, that's right three for £35. Be later tonight, bike trouble, address?' he said reaching out and tearing off a sheet from a police pad. They watched as he wrote it down. 'Don't drop me too close.' With a glance at the officers, he went to the table and started pocketing the drugs. The officers exchanged looks.

'What are you doing Ollie? said Mrs Lanesbury and turning to the officers.

'It's all right Mum, it'll be fine,' said Ollie touching her the shoulder. She looked up confused, her eyes moist.

'You can't sergeant,' said the female officer. Rawlins shrugged and went to the door. Ollie followed him out.

When Ollie alighted from the detective's car his legs weren't so steady. What would happen if the gang heard he had been arrested? Would they kill him? As he walked away, he remembered he had been stupid enough to keep the police guarantee on him. There was a slight drizzle, headlights reflected off the pavements in the darkening gloom of a winter evening. Going into the block of flats for his bike, he found two teenagers had removed it from under the stairs and were standing inspecting it. One in a heavy, hooded anorak was moving the handlebars. They must have just discovered it.

'Thanks,' said Ollie going straight to it and gripping the handlebars between the other boy's hands. The boy in the anorak tightened his grip. 'My bike,' added Ollie as he stared into the other's eyes. It was difficult to see them under the hood or what the boy was thinking but while they were no taller than Ollie, there were two of them.

'Oh yeah,' said the other boy.

'Finders keepers,' said anorak.

'Going to nick it were you?'

'Shouldn't be in here. Got to be confiscated.'

Ollie tried to pull the bike away, but the boy hung on. What could he do? He glanced around. Should he shout out, but he couldn't cause a scene, not with pockets full of crack. He heard footsteps at the top of the stairs and waited. A man, talking into the handsfree mike attached to his earphones, was slowly coming down. The stalemate continued.

'Right, I have to go, so get off,' said Ollie loudly and gave the bike a great jerk, stepping right into the path of the new arrival. Ollie and the bike banged into the man.

'Hey,' shouted the man, swinging round, fists clenching. 'You try anything.' The other boy let go.

'Sorry, just going,' said Ollie, pushing through the door leaving the others glaring at each other.

As soon as he had pedalled a few hundred metres he stopped. Removing the pieces of paper with the three addresses he reminded himself that he'd only been held for two hours. Surely, they couldn't have found out by now. Another customer rang.

It was 11.30pm by the time he returned to number 47.

'You're late,' said Maggie opening her eyes and yawning. Baz unfolded himself from another chair.

'Puncture,' said Ollie emptying cash and the last unsold packets on the table. 'It's all there.'

'Word is, the pigs picked you up.'

'My lights weren't working. Gave me a telling off and a lecture about safety. That delayed me plus the puncture; I need some new tyres.'

'They didn't search you?'

'I was frightened they would but why should they?' said Ollie looking at the floor. With an effort he straightened up and looked her in the eyes, 'I was just a white kid on a bike.'

'Alright,' she said, screwing her lips up in indecision and holding out forty pounds. 'Buy yourself some tyres.'

'Thanks,' he said.

School felt very peculiar. Nothing mattered anymore. He felt he was floating in limbo. A place where he had no control, just waiting for fate to strike. He rehearsed in his mind all the things that could go wrong. As he walked the corridors of school, every look, every stare threatened. Of the 1200 pupils he only knew a few. Any of the older kids could be sent to get him. How had they heard about the police, what else would they find out, would he be walking into a trap?

At home in the evening he waited, but no call came from number 47, no crash as a gang broke the door down. As he wore the carpet out with his pacing his imagination built frightening scenes.

'Ollie sit down. You mustn't have anything more to do with it,' said his mother.

'But it's our only chance. A complete escape for Sasha,' he said standing looking at her. She appeared suddenly small.

'Just tell the police you are sorry and can't do it.'

'But it's the only way.'

'It's too dangerous. These people -.'

'I'll be alright. They won't get me,' said Ollie. Stupid thing to say but saying it and trying to quell his mother's fears quietened his own.

'I won't let you. You are still a child.'

'Mum, I'm in trouble. It's a way out and I can do it. Rawlins knows what he's doing.'

At 9pm his phone rang. Glancing at the clock Ollie licked his lips. Odd time to ring? The contact list came up, "Peter DS." His code for the detective.

'Hi,' said Ollie, 'No call tonight, they won't ring now.'

'Tomorrow, do you think?'

'Spect so, never can tell.'

'Alright. We're ready.'

The following afternoon he couldn't stop glancing at his phone, whether in lessons or in the corridor. He cut short a call from a friend, and as he walked home the only call was from his mum.

'I can't talk mum; they might ring any moment.'

'You mustn't go through with it. I've talked to a solicitor. They can't make you.'

'Course not, but we have to and I'm ringing off. It'll be all right mum, don't worry,' he said pressing the off button.

'What was that about,' said Abdullah who was keeping him company.

'Nothing really but mum gets worried. She thinks I'm getting in with the wrong crowd.'

'She's not stupid then. You're up to your eyes in it.'

'Yeah, two chances, escape or they do me in. Either way thanks for sticking with me.'

'Okay bro no prob.'

He reached home and spread out some schoolbooks on the table, the phone beside them.

'Ollie you've been reading the same page all evening,' said Mrs Lanesbury coming in from the compact kitchen.

'I've only been back twenty minutes,' said Ollie, looking more closely at the page. She was right he couldn't concentrate. He glanced at the phone, willing it to ring, to get it over with. Would the cops re-arrest him if he didn't help close the operation down? He tried to go through the plan in his head and what might go wrong.

'It's no good looking at your phone. When they ring, you can just tell them you aren't going. I'm not letting you.'

'Sorry mum but I have to. It's the only way.'

'You are under eighteen, a child. If I say you can't go, you can't. I'm doing tea for six o'clock,' she said turning to go back into the kitchen. The shrill ring cut through his stupor. For a moment Ollie hesitated, then grabbed it,

'Yeah, downs run tonight, get round here quick,' said the voice, probably Baz he thought. He stood up.

'No, you can't,' said Mrs. Lanesbury coming around to stand between him and the door but Ollie was stabbing at his phone. It seemed to ring for ages before it was answered. Then just an answerphone. Sweating he tried again. This time on the fifth ring someone answered.

'It's on; tonight,' said Ollie, glancing at the clock. 'I'll leave here in ten minutes and then walk, so be at Thompson street by 5.40 pm. It's two minutes to South Street from there. Can you be in position by then?'

'No problem, same Mondeo, don't go in, until you've clocked us,' said D.S. Rawlins breathing heavily down the phone.

'Okay,' said Ollie, hesitating, before ending the call.

'Ollie,' said Mrs Lanesbury, her voice rising in tone.

'I need something to eat,' said Ollie going to the kitchen. He took out a loaf of bread,

'It's no good, you're not going,' said Mrs Lanesbury as Ollie started cutting a slice of bread. The slice started thick but tapered out before the bottom. 'I'll do that,' she sighed, taking the knife from his hand. There are two cooked sausages, I'll make you a sandwich.'

Ollie opened a pack of crisps and munched them. 'The police will be everywhere; nothing should go wrong. They'll keep me safe.'

'Just make sure you do what they tell you.'

Ollie smiled; it was him telling them. He took a swig of milk and with a fat sandwich in hand went to the door. He stopped and didn't turn away when his mother kissed him.

'See ya.'

'Bye darling, be careful.'

At first, he walked quickly, but then, glancing at his watch slowed right down. As the sandwich threatened to fall apart, he stopped to finish it. He arrived at exactly 5.40 but there was no Mondeo or any occupied cars in the small street. He went and leaned against a wall. Unusually it was possible to see the odd star and the lights of aircraft flying overhead. He felt conspicuous but looking around there was no-where to hide. He glanced at his watch and then again. The minutes dragged on.

It was 5.50 before two cars pulled in suddenly. He recognised the Mondeo. There wasn't anywhere for the second car to park in the packed street. It had to reverse up. Ollie walked on a little, wanting to be away from the sudden activity. Two men alighted from the Mondeo, the same two who had trapped him. Ollie turned and walked away. The walking began to unknot his stomach. He tried not to glance back but couldn't help it when he turned into South Street. The policeman in scruffy jeans and worn leather jacket was still following. Being white he looked out of place. Baz stepped out of number 47 and waved.

'Hi Bros, back to the sea then,' said Baz giving him a hi -five.

'Yeah, same run, where you off too?'

'Just hanging around for some of the gang, then got a couple of local drops.'

'Wouldn't hang around if you're carrying,' said Ollie suddenly wanting Baz to get clear.

'No rush man,' said Baz who appeared to be looking at the man in the leather jacket who had stopped and acted as if he was trying to light a cigarette. Ollie gulped and stepped towards number 47. The door was opened by one of the two youths inside. Maggie looked up and started tapping her phone.

'Downs run, here's your fare,' she said. This time you bring the cash back. You cheat on us and I'll send Todd after you. He'll always find you, wherever you hide.'

Ollie went and leaned against a wall, trying to look relaxed but it didn't feel like it was working. The beat of his heart reverberated in his chest and he felt a warm flush rise up his neck. He knew neither of the two lads, who appeared to be suspiciously watching him. Instead of the old Nigerian, an older white man shuffled in carrying a bag. An obvious addict, who stood, looking lost. Maggie nodded to Ollie who stepped over and took the bag. The man didn't move.

Ollie needed the man to leave but he stood rubbing his hands together. Everything was going wrong.

'Well, what are you waiting for?' said Maggie.

'How much money will they give me?'

'£2,500.'

'You want me to count it?'

'Up to you, but if its short you pay, now clear off.' The man hadn't moved. Ollie still hesitated, looked at the youths and moved to the door.

'I'll have to come back here then?'

'Yeah, so get going.' Ollie opened the door and stood there. He could see no one. The bag in his hand had to stay in the house. 'Go on.'

'Just checking, as I saw someone hanging around earlier,' said Ollie. He waved the bag and then he saw one of the policemen. He gestured, pointed to the bag and went back inside.

'There's a white bloke in the street, watching,' said Ollie.

'Give the bag back,' Maggie hissed. 'Take it back to the flat, usual place,' she added to the old man.

'I'll come back in half an hour,' said Ollie, striding to the door. Going through the front garden he was pushed aside by several men. Two had police jackets. There was shouting and someone grabbed Ollie. He struggled to free himself.

'Let go. I'm clean.'

'Make it natural but let him get away,' said DS Rawlings running past. Ollie twisted and kicked, then found himself propelled through the gate and was running. He stopped a few streets away and waited. After about half an hour, Rawlins, in the Mondeo, drove up.

'Get in.' Two men in the back made room for him as they accelerated away. They were both in informal uniform. Ollie looked around.

'Is there a second car?'

'Everybody's busy and two of the team are sick. Us four can take your man, he hasn't got the gun now has he?' said the policeman beside him.

'No, he won't be armed but he's very strong. There's also a back way out if you climb a wall. He could get out either way,' said Ollie.

'We know about the wall, with two of us round the back and two at the front we'll be fine,' said Rawlins. 'I should have more men, but it wasn't possible. You stay in the car. A marked car is on its way for our man.' Ollie looked at the four policemen. None were particularly big.

'I hope you are right.'

They stopped the car opposite the door, hard up against the bumper of Todd's BMW. The two in the back walked around the back of the house carrying a telescopic ladder. After a conversation on the radio, Rawlins walked up to the door with his uniformed assistant. Ollie sank down low but just high enough to see. When Todd opened the door. Rawlins held up his badge and without hesitation, Todd hit him in the midriff. The senior policeman collapsed, the other copper grabbed at Todd, but he twisted around, forced the officer's arm up, bent it at a nasty angle and threw him across the road. He ran to the Mondeo. Ollie ducked down low. After a glance at the empty ignition Todd dashed away.

The policeman limped to the car, talking on his radio. Rawlins had pulled himself up the doorway and gone into the house. With a last glance in the direction Todd had run, Ollie opened the car door and went to the front door.

'Sit down madam, I'll have a female police officer here any minute. Then you can tell us where your man might have gone,' Rawlins was saying.

'What are you doing here Ollie?' said Sasha.

'Helping put a murderer behind bars.'

'You grassed on us?' spat Sasha.

'Your brother was arrested carrying class A drugs, but that's not so serious as holding or hiding a murder weapon,' said D.S. Rawlins. 'It's time to come clean. We know Todd is very dangerous and that you are in danger whatever you say. Your only chance is to tell us all you know, now! Then we can protect you.'

'No comment and you get him out of here,' said Sasha pointing at Ollie.

'But Sasha, the police will protect us. Give us a new life away from here.'

'Oh yeah. Don't trust em.'

'Right Ollie, its time you went as I need your sister to come to the station and answer some questions.'

'No chance,' said Sasha.

'Just questions, otherwise I'll have to arrest you.' She shrugged. Okay I'm arresting you for withholding information -.' Ollie looked around the kitchen wondering at what he had done as the policeman finished his caution. A uniformed officer arrived with another man carrying a leather bag.

'But what about some protection? I can't just go home with Todd loose,' said Ollie.

'You'll have too. Your sister will probably be held overnight, and we will try to sort something for you tomorrow or by the weekend.'

'But you promised.'

'And we will get there, but your sister is going to the station now, so you can clear off home,' said D.S. Rawlins as a female officer walked in. Outside Ollie stood looking at the street. Two marked police cars were badly parking, calling attention to the house. A woman with two children stood watching. He ducked his head and hurried away. Scanning the next corner, he broke into a run. His heart was racing by the time he was twisting the key in the lock of the flat.

'Ollie you're back,' said his mum, stepping into the hall, her face tight with worry lines, 'you alright?'

'Just about,' he said putting the safety lock on the door. Not that it would be much good against Todd he thought. One good shove and it would snap. He took a stall from the kitchen and wedged it under the handle. It wobbled but might help.

'What's the matter dear?'

'The fools couldn't hold Todd, he's on the run.'

'Have you seen Sasha, is she all right?'

'Yeah, she's fine except she's not talking to the police. They took her in.'

'Oh no.'

'Mum, could you pursued her to tell them what she knows?'

'If you won't listen to me, she definitely won't.'

Ollie couldn't sleep that night, and in the morning, he couldn't decide what to do.

'You might be safer staying at home,' said his mum. 'I can take a day off work.'

'No, I'll go, my escape during the raid must have looked okay, and Todd didn't see me,' he said. The idea that his mother would stay home to protect him made him smile and had made up his mind. He picked up his phone and rang Abdullah.

'Wanna walk in via my home?'

'Yeah runnin late, see ya in a minute.'

School was uneventful. The drug raid wasn't a topic of conversation and for some of the time, Ollie forgot his troubles. He was careful however, to walk home with Abdullah. They hadn't gone far when they saw three teenagers sitting on a fence. Ollie shuddered but kept on walking head down.

'Don't look, but do you know any of them,' he whispered.

'Yeah the kid in the hoodie and the white kid used to go to our school before they got expelled,' said Abdullah.

'The one in the hood, do you know his name?'

'James something. I can find out from my brother if he's conscious. Why?'

'Better not say but if your brothers at home can you ring me. It's important.'

'Okay. I'm going over to Garry's house tonight. He's got some new games in. Do you want to come?' said Abdullah.

'Yeah okay, if we go together' said Ollie. A few games with some friends sounded wonderful, no more nasty calls.

'I'll come round at about eight then,' said Abdullah.

Over dinner his mother chatted on about nothing.

'Did you find out about Sasha?' Ollie eventually asked.

'Been charged with supplying A class drugs and she's going to court tomorrow,' said Mrs Lanesbury, after some hesitation as if it was something, she couldn't bare thinking about.

'That wasn't part of the plan,' said Ollie. His phone rang. It was D.S. Rawlin's number. He looked at it, should he answer? He better had.

'Yes sergeant,' said Ollie. 'Why have you charged Sasha?'

'Because she's guilty and hasn't been helpful. We need some statements from you too. Need you to come in after school tomorrow and come to the station?'

'Have you trawled up the gun yet?'

'No, but a diver has been at the river all afternoon, it better be there.'

'I saw the guy who did the stabbing today. Should have a name by tomorrow.'

'Good, I need that urgently. So far, all I have, is a few ounces of crack and four arrests. We are taking the storage flat apart, but we haven't found the main stash.'

'And have you caught Todd?'

'Not yet, but we will.'

'Until he's locked up, I'm -,' he hesitated, 'yes I'm scared. Can't be seen walking into a police station, can I? When will you have a safe house for us?'

'We are working on it, but I need your statements. I took a big gamble letting you go like that and I need a bigger case to get approval for the cost. Not cheap setting up a new start, I could pick you up from school in my car.'

'Half the kids would know you're a cop,' said Ollie, 'No meet somewhere busy. I know, in the high street outside Tesco's, say 4.20pm.,' said Ollie. He heard Rawlins mutter something as he put his phone down.

Ollie turned off his computer with a sigh. He just couldn't concentrate on homework or even a game. A knock on the door made him jump. He hesitated at the door.

'Who is it?' he shouted.

'Me. Who do think?' came Abdullah's muffled reply. 'You're really in trouble, aren't you?'

'Yeah well, I might be. You can never be too careful; I'll get my coat.'

Chapter seven. Trapped

It was another dark night, with occasional flurries of rain, the wet roads reflecting the lights of passing cars. The pavements were empty because it was a night to be inside. It was good to chat with Abdullah about normal things, but Ollie began to have a growing unease in the deserted streets. He should have stayed at home. Guilt feelings of involving Abdullah, and his own fears increased.

'By the way, the guy in the hoodie is called Hussain,' said Abdullah.

'Well done. Is it far?' said Ollie looking around again. Had someone behind them, stepped back into the shadows?

Abdullah stopped at a junction. 'I'm getting lost, Look it up on your phone will you. I stupidly left mine at home.'

With a quick glance around Ollie eased his phone out. 'Post code?'

'Dunno. Cambridge Street. Hey,' shouted Abdullah as Todd ran out of the darkness. Ollie turned.

'Run,' he squeaked but Abdullah was already leaping away. A hand grabbed at Ollie's shoulder, but he jumped to one side dropping his phone which bounced into pieces on the road. Then he was running in blind panic. The clatter of footsteps echoing off the buildings. He followed blindly wherever Abdullah lead, his mind frozen in fear. They needed people, crowds, not lonely streets. The pound of Todd's footfalls just behind began to recede. A quick look showed that Todd wasn't keeping up. Another turn, and for a moment he was out of sight. Ollie caught up with Abdullah who had stopped and was bent over.

'Phew, can't keep this up,' gasped Abdullah.

'Don't stop,' said Ollie running past.

'Can't go on.'

'Come on quick.'

They ran down the road, turned a corner and were out of sight again.

'Over the fence,' hissed Abdullah, throwing himself at the six-foot-high plywood and pulling himself up and over. The painted fence with its safety notices, and pictures of comfortable living in superior flats, surrounded a half complete hi-rise. Ollie stopped, hesitated, and then heard heavy footsteps drumming on tarmac.

He leapt for the top edge. Knees and trainers scraped the wood, as with an effort, he pulled himself up. For a second, he was balanced on the top and then he jumped, muddy ground softening his fall. Abdullah was crouching below the lowest scaffolding walkway which was only a metre above the ground. He put his finger to his lips. Ollie joined him and they both listened, holding their breath, not daring to move. The footsteps stopped. They sensed, rather than heard, Todd walk to the temporary mesh gates further on, that served as an entry to the site. The violent jangling of the gate chain made both boys jump.

'Only place the little bastards could have gone.' There was more rattling of the gate as if someone was trying to squeeze through, then silence. Bang, the ply fence shook, and Todd was over. For a moment in the gloom he didn't see the boys. Then . . .

'Got ya,' Todd shouted. Ollie leapt away, around a cement mixer, over a pile of sand and stumbled into a stack of rough timber and scaffold tubes. Abdullah just behind him cried out. Todd had caught his jacket and with a flick thrown him to the ground. Abdullah rolled close to the wall avoiding a foot lashing out at him. The second kick caught his forearm a painful blow as he sought to protect his face. His cry stopped Ollie, who, picking up a four-foot length of tubing from the pile of scaffolding, ran back. Todd was leaning under the scaffolding trying to reach Abdullah with his boot. The tube felt too heavy to swing.

With a stabbing action Ollie thrust at the man. His first blow brushed harmlessly off a shoulder. He had to hit harder, some-how he had to really hurt him; it was their only chance. Todd lunged at Ollie, straight into Ollie's second blow which caught Todd on the forehead. He grabbed the end of the tube and jerked it out of Ollies hands.

'I'm going to break every bone in your body,' Todd spat out. Ollie turned and ran. Terrified he knew he had to stay in the open. No getting trapped in half-finished rooms or stairs that ended with sudden drops. He reached a tall cement storage tower. It was about ten foot in diameter with little pyramids of set concrete at its base. In the half light from the streetlights, he could dodge to the right or left, always keeping the tower between him and his pursuer. The stalemate brought relief as had the fact he had hit Todd. Anger pushing the fear away.

'You'll think Sasha's injuries nothing, when I've got ya,' shouted Todd, wiping away the blood that ran down his forehead. For several minutes they danced around the tower, but Todd, was never near enough to catch him.

Ollie thought the impasse would eventually bring him safety, but Todd seemed as energetic as ever. Suddenly out of the shadows leapt Abdullah, swinging his own length of scaffold tube, which thudded into Todd's lower back. Todd stumbled, and Abdullah was several paces away before he could respond. He leapt after him, but Abdullah could run. Right round the building and back to the tower.

Ollie used the time to collect another piece of tube. He balanced its weight in his hands wondering if he was strong enough to swing it. Then Todd was back chasing them round the tower but there were two of them. One in front and the second boy trying to come around behind him and land a blow. Desperation gave them strength to swing the heavy tubes. They waltzed around, a frantic dance to hit out but not get within Todd's strong grasp.

In a moment when the streetlamp illumination was not obscured by the tower, Ollie saw that Todd was grinning. He was enjoying it. Even in his hatred, he was loving to fight. What were their chances? Then Abdullah caught a blow to Todd's legs. He staggered, but by the time Ollie was in a position to strike, Todd was up and ready. Dropping his own pole, Todd lunged and caught Ollie's, nearly dragging him within his grasp. Ollie fell in a desperate attempt to avoid the vice like grip. He rolled and kept rolling but Todd was swinging the newly gripped tube.

It smashed against the ground just inches from Ollie's head. There was another thud as Abdullah slammed a blow against Todd, who turned to retaliate but Abdullah's second downward strike crunched down on the man's collar bone. He stumbled and as Abdullah jumped away with Todd racing after him, Ollie was up, grabbing the scaffold tube to follow. He landed a blow on Todd's back, who stopped, turned and stood like some great bull. Solid and unbeatable.

'I'll kill you,' he snarled. Abdullah struck again and then Ollie was weaving in with another attack.

Like circling wolves, with sudden feints, and quick blows, they wore down their prey. It seemed to go on for ages, both boys careful not to become over-confident. Then with a last grab at them, Todd turned and ran for the fence, scrabbling up and over. He thudded on the pavement the other side.

'I'll get both of you, and your sister. You'll never know when I'm coming,' he shouted.

Ollie's legs were shaking, the trembling running up through his body. He shivered as his body heat dissipated and the sweat on his back turned icy. They collapsed on a pile of sand; all energy gone. The terrors began to seep away, he smiled, and leaned over and tapped Abdullah on the shoulder.

'You okay.'

'Yeah good,' There was nothing to say. They'd never forget the moment. 'Nasty bit of work.' They didn't have the energy to clamber up the fence, so they had to drag over an oil drum for a step up.

On the other side they looked at each other.

'Sorry Abdullah I think I prefer to go home.'

Abdullah grinned. 'You just can't take it can you?'

'I'm sorry I got you involved.'

'Cool man,' said Abdullah giving Ollie a hi-five.

They sauntered back, initially full of confidence but as they drew nearer Ollie's home their steps sped up. Where was Todd now? How could they all stay safe?

The rest of the evening Ollie sat slumped in front of the TV, went to bed early, yet still slept. When his mother knocked on his door at 7.30 in the morning, he shouted that he wasn't going in, turned over and went back to sleep. He didn't rise till eleven, pottered around, caught up with homework and wondered whether he ought to ring Rawlins. He rang from his mother's phone. It was eventually answered.

'Could be outside Tesco's earlier if you like?' he said.

'Yeah, okay 2.30pm.'

Standing watching the busy shoppers Ollie wondered how a new life would be and how would the police keep their new address secret if they had to keep going to court. Rawlins didn't turn up till nearly three.

'You're late,' said Ollie, jumping in.

'Some of us have been busy. We picked up Todd at dawn,' said the detective as they drove away.

'Whuhoo, that's great,' exclaimed Ollie. 'You had enough men this time?'

'Armed officers too.'

'Pity you didn't have an excuse to shoot him,' said Ollie as he remembered the thud of the scaffold pole by his head.

'Yeah, perhaps, although someone else had beaten him up, Bruises all over his body and a broken collar bone. I don't suppose you know who?'

'Might do but I can't say.'

'Did you get the name?'

'Yes, James Hussain. Will this take long?'

'Couple of hours.'

But it was gone eight by the time Ollie left. Sasha was being kept in, but she had begun to open-up, and the police said they wouldn't contest bail.

Ollie and his mother were at the magistrate's court the following morning. As they were waiting a female officer came up to them.

'Are you Ollie?' she said.

'Yes, why?'

'I'm told to tell you, we found the gun, but your sister is still holding back. D.S. Rawlins needs her to be a proper witness.'

'What am I supposed to do?'

'I don't know but he thought you might persuade her.'

Ollie sighed, 'Some chance, she's hardly talking to me.'

'But that's what we need,' said the woman as Sasha came out of the court.

Chapter eight. Brighton.

Little was said on the way home. Even their mother's attempts at small talk quickly died. While the other travellers on the bus looked at their phones or let their gaze take in the adverts and route, Sasha stared ahead as if in some other place.

Ollie decided it was not the time to talk and watched the other passengers and wondered at their lives. Perhaps it would be a mistake to leave the buzz of the great city, but they could never be safe here after they had given evidence.

'Right,' said Mrs. Lanesbury as soon as they reached the flat, 'I'll get some lunch, shall I?' Probably relieved to escape to the kitchen, thought Ollie as he and his sister sat wrapped in the cold silence. He sighed.

'What was it like, being inside then?'

'Dire, especially when it's your kid brother who dobbed you in.'

'But Sasha, you had to get away before he broke all your bones, and I couldn't get out either. It was the only way.'

'What, put Todd away for life. That's what he'll get if they can fix it on him.'

'He was flogging crack. You ever seen a crack house?'

'Nobody needs to buy it less they want it. I never tried coke, even when Todd offered.'

'Did he?'

'Sometimes, but he never took it. It was just business. He bought that house outright. There's cash hidden all over the place. The pigs will find it and I'll never see any of it.'

'It's dirty money.'

'Yeah, but drugs aint that bad, it's the turf wars that cause the problem.'

'You think crack's okay?'

'It don't do no harm. It's being a grass that stinks, so where am I going to sleep in this scruffy little flat?'

'Alright, I said I'd move into the box room,' said Ollie rising. 'I only did it for you.'

'Yeah, well keep out of my business in future.'

'Are you going to help the police? To testify?'

'No way. They aint going to let me off whatever they tell you. You're only a kid, a sort of victim. They'll treat you okay cause you'll only go to reform school or something, anyway. Me, I'm an adult. If they find prints on that gun, I'm stuffed.'

'If you don't become a witness, they won't give us a new life.'

'If I snitch on Todd in court, he'd find me where-ever I went.'

'What about crack, did they find any at your place?'

'Dunno, but if they did, they haven't said. Probably spring it on me. I can always say it's for our own use.'

'You used to deliver it for Todd?'

'Yeah, coke mainly, yuppy snow, the boys did the crack.'

'Yeah, free samples until you're hooked.'

'Their fault. If you can't control it, you shouldn't start.'

'What happened to the Sasha who used to care for other people?'

'Drugs aint that bad.'

'Soup's ready,' called Mrs. Lanesbury. As they ate, Ollie wondered at how Sasha had changed.

'When was the last time you saw the sea?' he said putting his spoon down.

'It's February,' said Sasha.

'But its stopped raining. You could do with some fresh air.'

'You need to clear the box room.'

'Later, we need an outing.'

'Yes, go on,' said Mrs Lanesbury. As Ollie munched his slice of cheese on toast, he thoughtfully watched Sasha.

'An afternoon by the sea, come on. I've enough cash for the rail fare.'

Sasha rose and Ollie was handing her, her coat and bundling her out of the flat before she had time to change her mind.

'I don't know why we are doing this, it'll be dark in a few hours,' she said as they found a seat on the train.

'You'll enjoy it, like old times,' said Ollie who reasoned that for so long she had done what she had been told, that if he kept on at her she would do what he said.

In the winter sun the waves crashing on the Brighton shingle were a different world.

'Come on,' he said, grabbing her hand and running to where the growling pebbles were being sorted by the ebb and flow of the surf.

'Lookout,' she cried as the next wave surged towards their trainers. They jumped back and continued along the beach edge, dodging each incoming breaker, their shoes ever at risk from the foaming water. They threw a few stones in the sea, then wondered back to the pier. In the amusement arcade they competed on a car racing game.

'How do we find The Lanes,' said Sasha as she watched Ollie's score match hers.

'Dunno, what's that?'

'Lots of cute little shops. Bet it's not far,' said Sasha. Ollie happily followed her. They didn't have the money to buy anything, but they still explored several of the shops before they closed. Lights were coming on, adding to the charm of the narrow streets. They came to the end and stood eating ice cream cornets, their only purchase. It felt quite natural even in the cold evening.

'We better go home,' said Sasha, 'or mum will be worrying.'

'Yes, but there is just one last place to go,' said Ollie, 'It's not far from the station. I think I know the way.' Sasha followed without comment.

'It's been nice to be away from it all,' she said.

'That's why you need to testify.'

'That will only make it worse. Why aren't we going to the station?'

'You'll see,' said Ollie as they turned down a side road, 'It's not far.'

'What's not far.' He didn't answer but kept on walking.

'Pleasant houses, aren't they?' he said before stopping in front of an Edwardian town house and looking up,

'Come on in and see what it's like inside.'

'But why,' she said following. He pushed the door open. A bleary-eyed man looked up from where he sat leaning against the wall. He didn't move as they stepped over his legs. There was a scream and shouting from the nearest doorway. Inside the room two women were spitting and snarling at each other like a couple of cats. A man was trying to separate them. He tried to gesture for help, but he needed both hands to keep the women apart. As much as they all swore at each other, the fight seemed in slow motion as if even in their hatred they hadn't the energy.

'This must have been a lovely room,' said Ollie in a raised voice. He sniffed the aromas, of damp walls and stale smoke. Seen from the shadows of the one bulb, the peeling wallpaper, cracked plaster, and graffiti were far from lovely. Only the Edwardian cornices were witness to the house's elegant past if the smoke yellowing was ignored.

'What are we doing here,' said Sasha again. Two scruffy newcomers shuffled into the room. One was male, the other they couldn't decide. The person was very thin and held a blanket tight around himself. Long straggles of unwashed black hair ran down the back

'Just thought you ought to meet some people,' he said taking her hand and walking out and into the next room. One teenager was pacing up and down, another was hunched over, holding a teaspoon of powder over the flame of his lighter, a third stood watching as if mesmerised.

'Right, let's see who's upstairs,' added Ollie dragging Sasha with him.

'No, I don't know why you brought me here, but we are in enough trouble without being mixed up with this lot.'

'Need to find Jenny. She's normally okay.' He pushed open the door to a small bedroom. The sheets unmade and rumpled gave off a stringent odour. 'No one here.' In the next room he saw her sitting head in hands. Two other people sat propped against the wall. 'Hi Jen, you alright?'

'Bad trip. What you doing here? Heard the pigs closed you down,' said Jenny looking up through bloodshot eyes.

'Just passing, wondered how you were doing without my deliveries.'

'Plenty of stuff about, but nasty additives.'

'You were a teacher weren't you, before you were introduced to snow.'

'Yeah, that soon stopped it.'

'This is my sister. She reckons a little crack never hurt anybody.'

'I didn't say that.'

'Keep away, it's the sweet poison that destroys yer.' Sasha turned and went down the stairs. Ollie didn't catch up until they were in the street.

'Moralising bastard, aren't you?' she said.

'Look Sasha I just wanted to show you what a crack house looks like. What Todd's stuff does to people.'

'Alright I get the message but I aint going to testify.'

Nothing else was said as a train was just leaving, and they had to run. When seated Ollie sat staring out into the darkness.'

'You know it's the right thing to do,' he eventually said.

'But its Todd, I'm terrified of what he'd do,' she said as she tried to scratch inside the inside of her caste with one finger.

'He'll be locked away for a long time.'

'Aren't you scared of him?'

'Not like I was. Not after he trapped me and Abdullah in a building site.

'What!'

'Two kids against a lunatic. For every bruise he gave you, we gave him two.'

'You're lying.'

'Nope, I thought he was going to kill us but Abdullah's very quick with an iron bar. Todd ran from us in the end.'

'But he's strong as a bear.'

'Yeah, but we struck like a couple of bees, buzzing and stinging. You get up in the witness box and tell the truth and we'll get a new life. I'm a witness in something else too, a stabbing, I wouldn't like that guy to come after me either but after Todd nearly killed us, I told myself I'd never be scared again. You might find the court interesting, enjoy being the star witness.'

'Huh.'

The small room was packed with stuff. He stared discontentedly at it. Where could it all go? As he moved it around, he found some photo print outs, some teddies of Sasha's and her artwork from school.

'Hey Sasha, come and tell me what you want done with all this stuff. Your paintings were very good,' he said holding up a garish painting of a Heinz baked bean tin.

'I suppose it better go in the rubbish.'

'But it's good. Will we be able to take any of it with us anyway?' By the time the space was just big enough for the futon to be placed in the middle it was late, and Ollie just collapsed on the little bed still surrounded by the debris of their lives. He tried to think back, to how it had for many years, been his bedroom. How had he coped in somewhere so small? He slept well and was having a late breakfast when there was banging on the door. Mrs. Lanesbury was already at work. Sasha still in pyjamas came into the kitchen. They both looked at each other. Ollie went to the door but didn't open it, leaning his hand on the stool that had been left jammed under the handle to make sure it would withstand an attack on the door, he called out.

'Yes, who is it?'

'Rawlins, I haven't got all day.'

'Okay,' said Ollie starting to move the stool and unlock the chain.

'I couldn't get you on your phone,' said Rawlins and I need you for an identification parade this morning.

'It got smashed up.'

'Then you need another,' said the detective and then he noticed Sasha standing watching. 'And you girl, are you ready to complete your statement?'

'Might be, but I need some stuff from the house, clothes and things.'

'We are still searching it.'

'You can carry on. I just need to rescue a few outfits before you ruin them.'

'Okay but you will have to come with your brother now and I'll get a female officer to drive you out from the station.'

'When will the new place be ready,' said Ollie going back to the table and spooning down the last of his cereal.

'We are working on it.'

'I haven't told the school why I'm off either. There's stuff in my locker at school.'

'Later, we need to go now.'

When they arrived at the station, Ollie & Sasha followed the detective who led them through to a small office. As he pushed open the door a middle-aged man arose from his desk.

'John, this is Ollie Lanesbury. You should have the case details. Now Ollie, John here, runs the identity suit.

He's not a policeman but it's his job, to show you a lot of pictures. He'll look after you, and you girl, you come with me and I'll get you a lift to the house.' As they left, the man gestured to a chair.

'Now Ollie, I'm going to show you a lot of pictures, one after another. If you see anyone you recognise, just stop me and we will make some notes. The tape recorder will be on, and the door open but if you want a female officer here, I can call one.'

'No that's fine,' said Ollie clearing a dry throat. This was the moment he committed himself. After that he would be hated, and they would be out to get him. Perhaps they wouldn't be recognisable anyway.

'We may have video footage as well but let's see what you make of these,' said John, opening a box of large photos and handing one to Ollie. They were all young men of mixed ancestry. Some of the pictures were standard arrest ID photos, others could have been taken from fashion shots. When he turned over the fourth one, he stiffened, James Hussain stared back at him.

'That's him. James Hussain the one who dropped the knife.'

'You sure? When did you see him?'

'At the murder street.'

'Okay keep going,' said John, typing into a laptop.

'Who am I looking for now?'

'Just keep going. There are over fifty pictures and you can go back if you need to.' Ollie continued, wondering at the people in some of the ID photos. What had they been arrested for? Had they sorted their lives, or had they become used to arrest, prison and being caught up in the legal system. He stopped, hesitated and stared at an ID photo. Baz, with number and date of arrest.

'Do you recognise him?'

'Well yes, but he was nothing to do the stabbing.'

'You sure?'

'Yeah, he was involved in the drug deliveries but he's a decent bod.'

'Keep going,' said Mathews putting the photo to one side.

'Ah, this is the other guy who nearly knocked me over.'

'Right, next one.'

'That's it, I won't remember any more.'

'Ollie, just keep going to the end. Take your time but be careful not to try to find faces.'

'Okay.' Who were all these people? Did they know that someone was using them as comparison for a murderer? He didn't expect to find anyone relevant so towards the end he was just glancing at them and putting them in a pile. The picture was second to last, which as he put it down, something made him want a second look. He picked it up again. A vision of that night, a tall black youth, standing a head height above the crowd, shouting as they gathered around their prey.

'I think he was there too.'

'Are you sure?'

'Not 100%, but pretty sure.'

'Mm, you're not trying to find anyone for the sake of it?'

'No, I can see him alright.'

'Well alright then. Another look through?'

'No that's fine, there won't be any others.'

'Ok, do you want a cup of tea and biscuit or orange juice or something, while I type this up?'

'Yes please.'

'Good work. D.S. Rawlins may want to talk to you, but I'll write this up for you to sign. There's something else to look at too but you need to go into the main office. Follow me.' Ollie was introduced to a female officer, who picked up a phone and gestured for Ollie to sit.

'Now stay here until I've typed up your identity statements which you will have to sign,' said Mathews. A cup of tea and some biscuits arrived and then a uniformed sergeant, carrying a clear plastic bag with a label attached.

'Do you recognise it?' said the policeman, holding out the bag with its hunting knife inside.

'Yes, that's it.'

'Sure.'

'Yeah.'

'But in your statement, you said it was a cowboy knife.'

'The only time I've seen anything like that was on TV, in old cowboy movies. What is it then?'

'Norwegian hunting knife.'

'Cool, where did you find it?'

'Can't say.'

'What will happen now.'

'Crown prosecution service will write up the case and it will go to court, but it may be months away.'

'Won't he plead guilty now?'

'No, the evidence is strong but not so strong that some lawyer won't try to get him off. Your evidence is key and you're a minor. You can probably give yours on a video link, but they will still try to undermine it, but nothing to be frightened of.'

The safe house didn't happen as promised and the two rooms in a Premier Inn in Woking while modern were very restrictive. For Ollie it was a decent school, however some of the lessons were at a different point of the curriculum. He found it hard to catch up. Sasha did some waitressing and Mrs Lanesbury obtained some agency work and they were given further financial assistance. D.S. Rawlins assured them it was only temporary until the cases were over. The threat of the prosecution to come was never far from their thoughts and conversations.

Chapter nine. Trial.

A date for the trial of Hussain and four other gang members drew near and then Ollie was meeting the barrister the day before, at a solicitor's office near the Old Bailey. He didn't sleep well over night and Mrs Lanesbury and he arrived on time for the ten o'clock appointment and were ushered into a meeting room panelled in light wood.

'Nice isn't it?' said Mrs Lanesbury, looking around after an assistant had gone off to get her a coffee. Ollie poured himself a glass of water from the jug in the centre of the table and took a biscuit. 'You shouldn't help yourself.'

'It's alright Mum, they're for us.'

'You nervous?' she said.

'Just a bit.'

'Ah, Ollie Lanesbury, and your mother,' said a woman swiftly walking in and holding her hand out. Ollie shook the woman's hand, regretting immediately his weak handshake. He hadn't expected a woman.

'Thanks for coming, I'm Jane Mathews the prosecuting barrister. I needed to meet you briefly, just to understand your story and make sure there are no hiccups. The trial starts tomorrow, Tuesday, but you won't need to be there, not until eleven on Thursday. The opening statements will take up the first day and most of the second. You may not be called, even then, however you need to be in court, just in case it all goes quicker than expected.'

'Are they still pleading "not guilty,"' said Mrs Lanesbury.

'Afraid so and because it's a conspiracy trial there are five defendants so five pleadings, a lot of sitting around. Are you worried?'

'A little,' said Ollie.

'This would be by video link which is normal now for minors.'

'But I'd much rather go to court.'

'Really! Well you are just old enough, but aren't you frightened?'

'Yes, I'm terrified but I've thought a lot about it. Ordinary kids get trapped in this gang thing unless people say what's going on.'

'Well, if you wanted to be present in person, it could only help the case. You may be asked to identify three of the prisoners when you will have to look at them, otherwise you can ignore them and direct your answers to the jury.'

Ollie gulped, 'How many people will be watching?'

'There's a lot of interest so public and press seats may be full but ignore them. However, the judge may restrict reporting so in fact it may be quite empty after all. In reality it's only between you, the jury, the judge and one barrister at a time; quite a small group really. You just relate to them. We mustn't rehearse what you could say but it's good to have an idea of what you might be asked.'

'The defence lawyer, what will he try to get me to say?'

'As you're a minor, the judge won't allow them to put much pressure on you. I have read all your statements and no-where does it suggest for instant, you were ever part of a gang. So, they might perhaps ask you whether you were, or have ever been a gang member,' was her first question. Others followed as the barrister went over every point. On Wednesday, Ollie was back at the new school. Not yet having made many friends, he didn't have to explain his absence. He presumed all the teachers had been told but he still had to explain that he wasn't going to be in, and could they give him some work to do at home.

On Thursday at eleven Ollie and his mother arrived at the Old Bailey and spent a panicky ten minutes finding the right court. Ollie, once he had met one of the prosecuting team and found out where everything was, settled down with his new phone. Occasionally someone came and went, then a large bewigged group flowed from the court.

'Hello Ollie, Mrs Lanesbury, we are adjourned for lunch. I don't think we will need you today but please join us for a sandwich,' said Jane Mathews. She looked very different in wig and black gown.

He wasn't wanted in the afternoon and even after they had been advised to be at the court by 9.30am on Friday he wasn't called until eleven-thirty. After he had been sworn in, the judge leaned over and said, 'Now Ollie, take your time and don't worry about everybody here.' Ms. Mathews rose,

'Ollie, please tell the court how old you are at what you were doing last January the 15th?'

'I'm fourteen and I had just come out of Earlsfield station,' said Ollie trying not to look at the defendants. He felt their hatred reaching out to him.

'Can you speak up please,' said the Judge.

'What time was this?'

'About ten o'clock in the evening,' said Ollie trying to stand taller and look at the jury. They were all looking intently at him, except one man who was fiddling with a notebook.

'What was the weather like.'

'Sort of misty rain.'

'Did that affect visibility?'

'Not at walking speed,' One of the jurors smiled and somebody in the gallery laughed.

'What happened then?'

'I had walked about 200 metres when I looked down a side street and saw a group of lads running up the street towards me.'

'Did you know any of them?'

'Yes, the one who was being chased.'

'You know his name?'

'Mo Darwish,' he said, one hand fiddling with the edge of the stand.

'Was he a friend?'

'Err, no.'

'How did you know him?'

'He supplied drugs and had tricked me into doing county line drug runs,' said Ollie. He felt sweat forming on his brow.

'Was he an enemy then?'

'Eh no, just someone to avoid if you could.' He rubbed his forehead with his sleeve.

'What happened next?'

'I turned to run and ran straight into someone else.'

'To help us understand the scene, where had this person come from?'

'He must have come up the other street and round to cut Mo off.'

'Objection, this is conjecture,' said another barrister rising. A tall man, with his wig set far back on his head. He looked austere, serious, not like the judge who appeared practically jovial.

'Is this someone in the court?' said Ms Mathews.

'Yes.'

'Can you point him out?'

'Number one.'

'In which direction was he running when he hit you?'

'Came up from behind me.'

'So that was the opposite direction from those running towards you?'

'Correct.'

'What happened then?'

'A large knife fell on the ground.'

'Please show Ollie exhibit three,' said Ms. Mathews. 'Do you recognise this?'

'Yes, it was the knife.'

'How can you be certain?'

'I had never seen one like this before, the bone handle with the black streak and the way the top of the knife curls.'

'In your statement to the police, before it was found, you described it as a cowboy knife. Why did you describe it like that?'

'I think I had seen knives like that in old cowboy films.'

'What happened then?'

'For an instant we stared at each other, then he picked up the knife and ran down to block Mo's escape.'

'Can we show Ollie exhibit 17,' said Ms Mathews. A plastic bag was brought over. He took it and looked at it carefully, turning over the small but heavy piece of gold.

'It is part of Mo's necklace.'

'And exhibit 18.'

'That is also part of another necklace that Mo wore.'

'Was he wearing them that night.'

'Yes.'

Gradually, painstakingly, every detail of the evening came out. Finally, Ms Mathews sat down, and the tall barrister rose. 'Which gang do you belong to?'

'I have never belonged to a gang.'

'But you have said that the boy Mo who was attacked that night was part of the gang supplying drugs which you delivered.'

'It doesn't work like that,' said Ollie, looking at his feet.

'How does it work?'

'I'm not sure really, but, while the gangs get their finances from selling the stuff on the street, they are just another retail outlet. The suppliers appear to supply dealers all over.'

'But this was a turf war that you were part of?' he said. Ollie looked at Ms. Mathews who didn't jump up and come to his rescue.

'I was never part of any turf war. This is just a guess on my part, but I think this attack was just a personal quarrel, someone disrespects someone else and they have to be attacked,' said Ollie looking up.

'You say you saw Mr. Darwish stabbed with the knife, but you also say he was surrounded by at least 15 people. One of those claims must be false.'

'No. I saw James Hussain block Mo's path, and then I saw the stabbing action from Hussain and Mo jerked and folded up. There was a second blow as the crowd surged round him.'

'But you didn't see the blade enter his body so it could have been somebody else who stabbed him? Or he was stabbed by others in the crowd as well?'

'I haven't seen the pictures of the injuries but perhaps if there were more than two.'

'I put it to you, that you were part of this gang and part of the attack that happened? That you are only here to cover your own crimes?'

'Do I have to answer this,' said Ollie, turning to the judge.

'I afraid you must.'

'Of course not. I've never been a gang member, never wanted to be or been forced to be.'

'You've never carried a knife?'

'Not a proper one.'

'Ah, you admit to carrying a knife?'

'Just a small penknife.'

'Why?'

'For doing all the little things you do with a penknife.'

'What's that?'

'Like opening things, sharpening pencils, and such like.'

'You never carried any other weapon?' said the barrister. Ollie hesitated.

'I was so scared I carried a screwdriver for a while, but I stopped,' said Ollie. The barrister was looking at his papers and didn't ask the expected question. 'I was so appalled at what I saw that night that I haven't carried it since, seeing someone stabbed makes you realise how horrible it would be to hurt someone like that.'

'No more questions,' mumbled the barrister sitting down. The judge nodded at a different barrister who was standing, a portly self-important sort of guy, thought Ollie.

'My client Mr. Abu Waseem was identified by yourself eighteen days after the incident yet denies being there and was not seen by anyone else at the scene of the crime. Could you tell the court how you can be so sure in that time that the man you saw was my client.

'I'm sure. He passed very close to me.'

'From your description you suddenly witnessed a very a frightening scene. Were you not shocked by what you saw?'

'Yes very.'

'How long did you watch the attack?'

'I have thought about it a lot since, but it is very difficult to judge. Possibly the actual attack about 90 seconds, watching Mo on the ground as they ran away, standing not knowing what to do, another couple of minutes.'

'So, in just 90 seconds, in a state of real shock you can be really certain that it was my client and not someone similar in appearance? Come on Ollie there must be some doubt in your mind?'

'No, none at all, the scene is etched on the back of my eyeballs. Close my eyes and I'm there; your client had on a grey hoodie and skinny jeans.'

'Ah, if he was wearing a hooded top, how could you see his face?'

'Because he ran into me. We practically rubbed noses,' said Ollie. There was laughter from the gallery. 'I also saw him clearly as he joined Hussain in the ruckus.

'But you didn't see him stab anyone?'

'No, he ran with Hussain to cut off Mo, and then grabbed Mo, who was then stabbed.'

'Just to confirm you didn't see my client with a knife or see him stab anyone?'

'No, he just held Mo so he could be stabbed by Hussain.'

'Um, well, why did you run away?'

'Thankfully people called the paramedics. There was nothing I could do, and I was frightened.'

'So, you just left your friend dying in the gutter.'

'I know, I've thought a lot about that too,' said Ollie studying the floor. 'He was no friend, but I should have gone to him.'

'No more questions.' Even as he was sitting down a further barrister was standing, a sheaf of papers in his hand.

'I represent Adam Kivu here,' he said, waving his papers. 'Now you have given a very clear statement regarding two of the defendants that you bumped into, yet from a photo you also suggested my client might have been there. You were unsure at the identity suite. On what basis in that 90 seconds could you have made any sort of clear and accurate judgement regarding the other lads who were involved in the melee?'

'He stood out, being rather tall, I think he was yelling.'

'You think? But you are not sure?'

'No, I am not completely sure but I'm pretty sure, 95%.'

'So, you do have some doubt.'

'Only a little, 5%.'

'It's not the percentage that matters but that doubt exists. A person must be convicted beyond all reasonable doubt. I put it to you, that your doubts make your identification unreliable and so should be dismissed.'

'I think it is clear enough to be added to whatever other evidence exists.'

'That is not for you to decide. The person you saw that night, who might have looked like my client, did you see him stab anyone?'

'No. As I said, I only saw one actual stabbing, the rest were just trying to catch Mo.'

'How far was this milling crowd from you?'

'I don't know, quite close.'

'Come on 60 metres, 100 metres?'

'When they caught him, probably only eight metres away?'

'But they didn't attack you? Threaten you?'

'Not directly, no.'

'And it was very dark and raining?'

'Light drizzle but there were streetlamps. I could see only too well.'

'You identified two different pieces of gold necklace, exhibits 17 and 18 as of the type the victim wore. Which was he wearing that night?'

'Both of them.'

'Two! Why would he wear both?'

'He always wore a lot of chunky gold like that, wrists, neck, rings everywhere.'

'No more questions,' said the barrister sitting down. The judge swept his gaze across the lines of barristers.

'We will adjourn till Monday morning, I would remind the jury they must not speak to anyone about the case other than among themselves,' he said gathering his papers together and rising. There was a clatter of movement as everyone stood and as soon as the judge had disappeared, they began to leave. Ollie breathed out, noticed for the first time that his back was wet with sweat, but didn't move.

'Well done young man,' said a solicitor, and then Jane Mathews approached.

'You are done, that's it, all over, how do you feel?'

'Like a limp rag.'

'I'm not surprised but it couldn't have been better.'

'Is it possible to come up and see the rest of the trial?'

'Do you want to?'

'It's fascinating, so much careful detail. The wrong word could easily skew the jury's opinion.'

'Exactly; and asking a good witness a question when it's better not to. The defence would have been better to ignore you.'

'Will they be convicted?'

'Almost certainly, after today.'

'How do you become a barrister?'

'Very difficult, do you know there weren't any women barristers until 100 years ago.'

'Lots of studying I suppose.'

'Yes, but then you have to be accepted into one of the chambers, which is difficult if you don't know the right people.'

'Oh, so just for the privileged few.'

'It's getting better,' she said with a laugh, 'but I tell you what, if you ever do get qualified come and see me and I'll find you a place.'

Chapter ten. School.

'The head of house is off today so you'll have to see the headmaster,' said the receptionist at the Exeter school. She looked nervous, 'Please knock, but you mustn't go in until he calls you. Leaning forward she spoke into an intercom.

'Headmaster sir, that boy, Ollie Lanesbury is here, the one the police liaison officer sent.' There was a distant reply, and a click.

'Have you just moved to Exeter?' she whispered to Ollie.

'Yes, my sister and mum are going to work at the university.'

Ollie went and knocked and sat down to wait. He glanced at his watch. Children of all ages came and went along the corridor plus the occasional adult and all gave a sideways glance at Ollie, but no one spoke. He was wondering if he ought to knock again when he heard a gruff, 'come in.' Eleven minutes wait according to his watch.

'Come in boy. Don't dawdle. Now we are not sure if this school is right for you, we have very high standards. We understand you will have a great deal of catching up to do. The -.' He continued, probably the same speech he had churned out hundreds of times before. A tall man, watery eyes with dark shadows under them but he sat very straight. Ex-army thought Ollie. As the speech continued, Ollie looked past and out through the picture window. Two teams were playing hockey and on the far side of the wide field, a group was practising the javelin. That wouldn't have happened in his last school, no one would have dared to give the kids a javelin. His mind returned with a jerk to -.

'So, we think you'd be much better going to the comprehensive in -.' the headmaster was saying.

'I don't think so,' said Ollie interrupting. 'I'm sure your school would give me a more suitable education for the career I have in mind.' The headmaster adjusted his glasses as if looking at Ollie for the first time.

'More suitable! And what career is that?'

'I wish to be a barrister.'

'A barrister! I'm afraid that would be difficult, quite impossible.' He smiled. 'It is still a profession that is really only open to the privileged few.'

'You have a very good record here sir and your hockey team won the inter school trophy last year. Why don't you think your school could give me the education I need?'

'Well, our A-level results and university entrants are excellent but from there, just getting into a legal practice would be difficult. Ambition is to be admired but crushed hope can lead to much unhappiness.' Perhaps he had wanted to be a general thought Ollie.

'You get me to a good university, and I'll do the rest. I have been promised a place in chambers if I can get a good education and do well at law college.'

'Really,' said the headmaster with arched eyebrow. Perhaps he thought he had found another compulsive liar. He must have met plenty, some of them no doubt very good too. 'And what chambers is that?'

'Mid temple, Jane Mathews.'

'I see, but could you get on with the other pupils here?'

'I can probably cope with a few upper-class bullies,'

'Mm that's not what I meant. We don't allow bullying here.'

'No sir,' said Ollie but thinking, I bet it goes on.

'I understand you will have to take time off to give evidence in a further trial. That will also put you behind and the worries and fears from such an ordeal will not help?'

'It's important to keep it secret sir but I'm not really frightened, in fact I'm looking forward to it.'

'What, some sort of fame?'

'Oh no, but if people do terrible things, it's right they are punished. How justice actually works in practice is very interesting.'

'And what is justice, and does it work?'

'I'm not exactly sure sir, but without it the world becomes a vicious jungle.'

'So, if we gave you a place when would you wish to start?'

'Today, please,'

'Now! alright, well, err welcome then. I hope you will be happy here.'

'Thankyou sir, I'm sure I will.'

Printed in Great Britain
by Amazon

Printed in Great Britain
by Amazon